Angel of Gold

To Margurita

Angel of Gold

ENJOY

Y. Ron Sharoni

Y. Ron Sharoni

Sharodine Publishing
New York

PUBLISHERS NOTE: This is a work of fiction. Names, characters, places, and incidents are either the product of the author's imagination or are used fictitiously, and any resemblance to actual persons, living or dead, business establishments, events, or locales is entirely coincidental.

Cataloging-in-Publication Data has been applied for and may be obtained from the Library of Congress.

ISBN: 978-0-9791726-0-1

Cover art by Aaron Zimmerman
Illustrations by Rena Griffiths

Special thanks to Ari Weiss, John Zeller, Ben Abraham, and Candace Frede

Printed and bound in Canada

SHARODINE PUBLISHING

18 Haven Avenue
Port Washington, New York 11050

sharodine@gmail.com

www.AngelofGold.com

For my wife, Francine Frede.

Without you, this story would be in the drawer for another 13 years.

Thank you for your hard work in bringing this story to print.

ANGEL OF GOLD

CONTENTS

CHAPTER 1

ADAM AND MAGGIE

It was a sunny day in Goldstone, California, June 25, 1875. The light breeze made it seem cooler than the 90 degree temperature outside.

Adam Starks sprinted up a dusty dirt road to try to make it to the General Store before the 6 p.m. closing time. As he neared the store, a large log cabin, he saw a brown-haired girl, in a white blouse and an ankle-length skirt, stepping out of the store, locking the door, and walking away.

"Hey!" he yelled, breathing heavily as he ran. She didn't hear him. He remembered her name now from having heard it in the hallways of his small school.

"Maggie!" he shouted out. She turned around, and he saw her long, wavy hair bounce behind her. As he approached, he could see her sparkling blue eyes. She was pretty, with a kind face. He was completely lost in her beauty and didn't hear when she spoke.

"Oh, hello, Adam. What can I do for you?"

"Pardon me?" he asked.

"What is it that you want?" she asked again.

"Oh, sorry, I saw that you just closed the store, but I need to pick up a few things for my family for dinner. Could you open up for just a second?"

Maggie smiled. She thought Adam was pretty cute—tall and handsome, with dark hair and a sweet disposition. She could definitely do him the favor of opening the store again.

"Sure," she said, flipping her hair without knowing how much attention it drew. "But just this once." She winked at him and opened the door.

He thanked her and hurried to the back of the store, quickly grabbing what he came for. He returned to the front of the store and pulled out some money from his pocket but realized he was a little bit short.

"Hey," said Maggie, sensing he was a little embarrassed. "I'll just put this on your family's account."

Adam smiled, relieved. "Well, thank you again."

They stood smiling and looking into each other's eyes for what seemed to be a very long time. Adam sensed that he'd better say something while he had the opportunity, and so he asked, "Can I walk you home?" He had always wanted to get to know her at school but never had the chance.

Maggie smiled. She was happy to have his company on the way home, and she agreed. "As long as we're both going in the same direction, I guess it's okay."

And so the young couple—Adam was fifteen, Maggie fourteen—walked down the dirt path together.

As they walked through the busy town, they passed the Town Square, the saloon, the church and convent, Mr. O'Grady's Barber Shop, Ling's Chinese Laundry, the clothing and tailor shops, and old man Riley's blacksmith place.

There were several homes along the way, each having it's own personality but still mostly the same: a single-story wooden structure, with a small window right next to the front door. They weren't large houses, but they were big enough for the families that lived there.

In contrast to these homes, and the simple shops in Goldstone, was the Governor's mansion, which stood over the town on a nearby mountaintop.

The four-story stone house had elaborate roman columns and gleamed with gold filigree detailing. The majestic property was a constant reminder of the Governor's power and position.

As they began their walk, Adam and Maggie didn't talk much but took in the scenery. Adam wished that he had the courage to reach out to hold her hand. They hardly knew each other, but it felt like they had walked together this way many times before. They were relaxed in each other's company, and they started to talk about their friends and teachers at school, their families, and some of the people in town they both knew. Before long, they were at the door of Maggie's house.

As they approached, Adam turned to Maggie and asked, "Would you like to walk together to school tomorrow?"

"Yes, I would," responded Maggie. "Meet me right here at 7:45."

Adam walked home smiling from ear to ear with a light heart. He was sure that nothing in the whole entire world could bring him down from this high-in-the-sky feeling. But as he would soon find out, he was wrong.

Adam arrived at his house with the groceries in hand. He gave everything to his mother, Samantha Starks —a short, dark haired, slightly heavyset woman who looked older than her thirty-nine years. "I'll get dinner ready."

"Great, Ma," said Adam, as he sat down at the kitchen table, still beaming from his thoughts of Maggie.

Adam's father, James, looked over at his son and saw his sweet, smiling face. It made him feel terrible about what he had to say to him at this moment.

"Adam," he called.

"Yes, Pa?" Adam responded.

"I need to talk to you for a few minutes while mother gets dinner ready." James' voice revealed his uneasiness and the seriousness of the situation to be discussed.

Adam was a bit confused but left the kitchen table to follow his father to the porch outside.

"What's the matter, Pa?" he asked. Adam could sense the tension and see the concern in his father's face. James was rubbing his graying head, his brow was furrowed, and his shoulders, stooped.

"Son, you know that I love you very much, and I do everything I can to make sure that you, your mother, and your little brothers and sister have all that you need, don't you?" he asked. Adam nodded.

"And I know you would do anything for us, too, wouldn't you?"

"Well, of course, Pa," Adam responded. He always knew that the family would need him to help out sooner or later. "You want me to start working weekends or after school a few days a week. I can do that, Pa."

"Not exactly," responded James. "We are running out of money, son, and our credit is overextended. It's becoming hard for me to put food on the table, and we need extra income.

"I spoke with my boss, Mr. Fitz, and arranged for you to work at the mines for eight dollars a week. That's excellent wages for a boy your age."

Adam was stunned. He didn't know what to say. "But Pa, how is that possible? I have to go to school."

James looked down at the floor. “Son, I know this isn’t what you had planned, and you’re disappointed, but I left school when I was younger than you to go to work. If you think about it, Son, what would you do with all that education anyway? You’d be wasting your time, Son, sitting in the classroom. You’re young and strong, and it’s time you started working to help your family survive, put food on the table. We need your help, Son.”

Adam was now fighting back tears. “But Pa, I don’t want to live this kind of life, I want to . . .”

James interrupted his son, talking softly but sternly, and fighting back some tears himself. He didn’t want to make his son give up his dreams, but he was scared about the future and not being able to support his family.

“I’m sorry, Adam. I know this is hard. But life isn’t always about doing what you want to do. When I was your age, I always dreamed of owning a farm. But there was no way for me to make enough money to buy the land and support a family. I did my best, Son, but this is just the way things turned out.”

James was thirteen when his father, a struggling laborer in New York, first heard that gold had been found in California in 1848. The possibility of striking it rich seemed like the answer to all their problems.

They managed to scrape together the fare for passage by ship to the Isthmus of Panama, followed by a three-day canoe trip on the Chagres River to the Village of Cruces, transferring to mules for the ride to Panama City.

James' parents didn't complete the journey. His mother contracted cholera from the polluted water and died on the ship two weeks into the trip. His father was strickened with malaria from the mosquitoes in Panama and was also buried at sea.

James was an only child, and at this point in his life, he found himself alone in the world and on this final voyage from Panama to California.

He managed to fight his way onto the over-crowded ship and got on board. The ship to San Francisco arrived three weeks later. He then joined a wagon train to Sacramento Valley and went to work prospecting for gold, just as his father had planned to do himself. His entire life was turned upside down, but James managed to survive.

He panned for gold all day in the scorching sun, working into the night, when the wolves would be howling from the mountains—day after day, night after night.

Some had found their fortunes but not James. He finally gave up and travelled to the town of Goldstone, taking a job at the mines.

He didn't meet his future wife, Samantha, until six years later. She was a daughter of another miner.

With a steady job at the mines, he was able to build a life for himself, as people did in those days, as best he could.

He loved the land, and he loved his family. It broke his heart now to disappoint Adam, but he had no choice.

"Adam," James continued, "if there was anything else we could do, we'd do it, but I see no other way. I know it's not the life you wanted, and it's not the life I wanted for you, but we need to survive now, and the work at the mines is steady. It will put food on the table."

Adam let out a deep breath. He was crushed. But he saw the pain and worry in his father's kind eyes, and he understood. There was no choice. He nodded.

His father patted him on the back tenderly, knowing that he could count on Adam. "Good, Son," he said softly, "Just remember to listen to Mr. Fitz at the mines, and everything will be fine for us."

Adam couldn't sleep at all that night. He cried and cried, muffling the sound with a pillow so he would not wake his family.

At the first sign of morning, he jumped out of bed. After not sleeping a wink and all those tears, his eyes were puffy and swollen. Adam's world seemed hopeless and gray, and he wouldn't have even gotten out of bed or left his house to go to school that morning if it hadn't been for Maggie. He had such a longing to see her. She seemed to be the only bright thing left in his life.

He walked to her house rather quickly, but then slowed down as he got closer. He was feeling so badly, he walked with his head down, with a deep and thorough tiredness.

When he arrived at Maggie's house, she smiled at him. "Good morning, Adam. I'm glad to see you again—and you're early, too!"

Adam tried his best to match her excitement, forcing a smile. "Hi, Maggie; I'm really happy to see you." But his exuberance sounded forced.

Maggie could see from Adam's disheartened state and obvious fatigue that something was wrong.

"What is it, Adam?" she asked, as they started to walk toward school.

"It's nothing. I just didn't sleep at all last night, so I'm very tired."

"What kept you up, Adam? You can tell me."

"It's nothing, Maggie. I don't want to talk about it," he replied.

"I don't think it's nothing," said Maggie. "You sound miserable, and you look awful. And you couldn't sleep."

"It's nothing, Maggie. I'm fine. I'm sorry."

But then he couldn't hold it in anymore, and it all spilled out. "Today is the last day I'll be able to go to school." He paused and leaned on a fence near the intersection of Governor's Road and School House Road, just about twenty yards from the school. Maggie looked at him with concern. His eyes filled with tears as he began to explain.

"My father is making me work for Mr. Fitz at the gold mines. I know I should want to help my family, and we need the money. I don't want to think only of myself. But I don't want to end up like my father. He told me that he always wanted to have a farm, but he could never get out of the mines. He had to give up his dream for the family. Now it looks like I'll have to do the same. That's not fair, is it?"

Maggie put her hand on Adam's shoulder, unsure of what to say to try to comfort him. She couldn't explain it, but something about this boy touched her heart very deeply.

Adam continued, as tears fell down his cheeks. "I want to learn. I want to do something important. Now I'll never get out of this town. I'll just work for the rest of my life in the mines, scrape by, and die a poor, sad man!"

Maggie embraced Adam. She wanted to help him anyway she could. She spoke softly into his ear. "That's not the way it has to be."

Adam was still upset. "You don't understand, Maggie. I have no choice. There's no other way."

"No, Adam. I mean I won't let you be like the other miners, stuck in that dead-end life forever. You don't have to stop learning just because you won't be going to school anymore. I can teach you."

Adam wiped the tears from his eyes and smiled. In an instant, he felt hopeful again. "Really? Would you do that for me? Would you have the time? When would we meet? Where?" He couldn't contain his excitement.

They thought for a moment, and then Maggie said, "I know. Let's meet under the big willow tree. It's pretty quiet; no one ever goes there."

Adam knew the place; it was about a quarter mile outside of town. "I can meet you there right after school," she continucd.

Adam was so relieved and said, "That would be wonderful, Maggie." He was so happy at the prospect of seeing Maggie every day and continuing his education.

"Okay, then," she replied. "Let's meet after school today. We'll see if we like the place and make plans for next week."

"Thanks, Maggie. See you then."

CHAPTER 2

MR. FITZ

The weekend passed quickly for Adam. He spent all of his time thinking about how wonderful it was going to be to see Maggie. And then, Monday arrived, and it was time to go to work at the mines.

Goldstone Mines was run by Andrew Fitz, a rich, cunning businessman from Germany. He had abandoned his wife and two children to hide from debt collectors and seek his fortune. That was over twenty years ago, and he never looked back. He never panned for gold personally, nor worked in the mines, but he made his fortune during the Gold Rush.

His European connections enabled him to gain employment as a manager of one of the small mining operations. He was also a gambler and didn't mind cheating. Before long, he had enough winnings to buy the small mining company for himself.

When he heard of some overseas investors coming to the area to open a competing mining operation, Andrew Fitz knew he needed to form a partnership with them. It would be a quick way to expand his mining business and gain credibility and respect in the community.

With his experience and connections, Andrew Fitz was easily able to become a minority shareholder of this new, greatly expanded operation, and he immediately went to work on building the business.

Up until this point, he was known for his underhanded dealings and heavy gambling, as well as his iron-fisted ruthlessness at the small mining operation. And that was fine with Fitz, as long as the profits came in.

A short, fat, balding man, with moustache and goatee, he dressed the part of a gentleman. He was always on the lookout for the next opportunity to present itself, while running the largest business in town.

As gold fever swept across the country, a large settlement took shape in the valley. Schools were built, a Chinese laundry opened up, and families came from the East Coast, Europe, China, and elsewhere to make a new home. They named the town Goldstone.

For years, the town thrived, with its main industry being the gold—the economic heart of the community. Two of Fitz's friends from the gambling days, Harry Catcher and Peter Rays, were hired as security, and operations ran smoothly.

As time went by, Andrew Fitz made a name for himself in Sacramento and its neighboring towns. As his mining business grew, so did his reputation and influence.

Mr. Fitz was so influential that when Jeffrey Tannin decided to run for the office of Governor of California, he sought out Fitz's support. At the start of his campaign,

Tannin had been touring the state when he learned that an opponent had joined the race. His name was Colonel Stephen Saunders, and he was well known for his heroic actions in the recently won Mexican/American War.

The election for State Governor was to be in three months, and Tannin needed a plan of action to out-do his political rival. He was in Sacramento when he contacted Andrew Fitz; he looked forward to meeting the man who represented the rags-to-riches dream, the town's most prominent businessman.

Fitz had few connections outside of northern California; however, he did have ambitions to gain power, and he knew that political friends would help.

Andrew Fitz agreed to see him.

Tannin journeyed to Goldstone—a few hours east of Sacramento—and met with Mr. Fitz. They sat in the local saloon, while Tannin explained to Fitz, over a steak dinner, how he was hoping to be elected Governor of the State this year.

"My main concern, Mr. Fitz, is that my opponent, Colonel Saunders, will take a larger percentage of the votes based on his recent service to the country."

Mr. Fitz nodded. "I see."

"I have not been a man of the military but more of an independent thinker," continued Tannin.

"Yes, I understand," Fitz agreed. "A good politician need not be a man of battle. He can be a capable, free-thinking man of action."

"I can assure you that I am," Tannin asserted between bites.

"So, what can I do for you, Sir," asked Fitz. "I'm sure that if California thinks as I do—and I feel the vast majority does—you will surely be elected Governor." He casually took a sip from his glass of wine.

"Well, I was coming to that, Mr. Fitz. May I call you Andrew?" Fitz nodded.

"And may I call you Jeffrey?" Fitz asked.

"Why, of course, Andrew, please do. Now, I'm sure you know, you are primarily known for your successes up here in northern California, but I know that you have the potential to be recognized statewide, and even nationwide. You just need the proper exposure. That is, if you have the inclination, Andrew."

Fitz smiled. He enjoyed hearing the prospective Governor speak the words he longed to hear.

"Oh, I have the inclination, Jeffrey. I can assure you that I do," Fitz quickly replied.

"Well, then, Sir, I would like to call upon you as my aide."

"Hold on there," Fitz interrupted. "Are you saying you want me to work for you?"

Jeffrey Tannin cleared his throat. "No, Sir. Not exactly. Allow me to explain myself. If you back my campaign for Governor, Andrew, all of Goldstone will surely cast their votes for me, and Sacramento and the whole State of California will follow. You have a mighty presence, Sir, and I'd like to make use of your stature. We both share a common goal. We want to make it in this country, and we want to make it big. I can assure you that we will make it big together—each in our own way. And when I succeed, I'll be there for you. Give me your support, Andrew, and I will be forever in your debt."

Fitz was a gambler, but not when it came to his future. He liked the idea of having the Governor in his back pocket. You never know when you can benefit from political connections, he thought to himself.

And so, the conversation continued, and Fitz and Tannin struck a deal. Fitz was nobody's fool, and he made sure he had certain promises in writing.

Tannin won by a landslide when certain rumors started to circulate regarding Colonel Saunders and some cowardly actions on his part during military service. It didn't matter if the rumors were true or not—just the possibility and the unanswered questions brought him down.

Jeffrey Tannin knew that Andrew Fitz was a very powerful and resourceful friend, indeed.

Immediately after assuming office, the new Governor moved his base of operation to the town of Goldstone and built his mansion there, to be near the man who helped him win the election.

CHAPTER 3

THE GOLDMINE

Adam wanted to make a good impression on his first day at work and arrived early. Mr. Fitz was unimpressed and barely looked up when Adam came into his office.

"Good morning, Mr. Fitz. I'm Adam Starks."

Adam noticed Mr. Fitz's appearance. His fine dress shirt was soaked with sweat, and his vest was pulled tightly over his big belly.

Mr. Fitz said coldly, "Jack is waiting for you by the site. Go on now."

Adam turned and walked out of the office. Looking ahead, he saw the foreman wave to him.

"Hello, Adam. Good to see you."

"Good to see you, too, Jack."

"Welcome aboard."

Adam shook hands with his father's closest friend, and they walked toward the mines. Before long, Adam found himself being lowered on a pulley, along with the crew, as they descended down into the mine shaft.

They stepped onto solid ground and approached a cart sitting on a track waiting to bring them to the heart of the mine.

After arriving at their dig spot, the six-man crew began chipping thunderously at the sheets of rock within the cave with pickaxes.

Jack stood with Adam in front of the mining cart. The older man was instructing him on the mechanics of the job and introducing him to all the men.

"Adam, I think you'll be okay here," Jack said. "Your father has always been an excellent foreman, and I see a lot of him in you." Adam nodded and thanked Jack for his kindness.

"We usually work at the dig site until 3:15. Sometimes we use explosives to widen the area. We did that yesterday over here, so today we are ready to dig. You'll get a chance to work all types of equipment. At 3:25, we get back on the cart and head over to the pulley to take us back up.

"Then we change from our work clothes into our own clothes and get inspected before leaving. That's part of Mr. Fitz's security check.

"We usually get to go home around 3:30. If you have any difficulties, Adam, you come to me."

When Adam finished his first day's work, every muscle in his body ached. It was hard work. He had a quick dinner with his family, and then walked toward the willow tree to meet Maggie for his study lesson.

Maggie met him at the road, and Adam carried her books for her. They walked over to the tree and sat down.

"What was it like at the mines today?" Maggie asked.

"Everything went fine, I suppose," Adam replied, not wanting to complain about how physically difficult the work was. "My father's friend, Jack, is my supervisor. I like him very much. I didn't really get a chance to talk to the other guys. They're all older than me and have their own lives to worry about. But Jack told me about each person in the crew. Overall, I missed going to school."

"I know, Adam. It's not the ideal situation, but you have to accept that this will be your life for the next few years. Not forever, but just for now. So, let's start today's lesson."

Maggie opened a book and began reciting a math problem. She glanced at Adam and asked, "Are you listening?"

Adam didn't respond for a moment, caught up in the sudden realization that his new friend, Maggie, was the most beautiful girl he'd ever seen.

"Yes, of course," Adam finally exclaimed, and they continued the lesson. After an evening of studying, they walked home.

Adam woke up the next morning energetic to start the day. He rode to the mines and unsaddled his horse at the workers' stable. He then joined Jack on the cart which would take them down to the dig site below.

The day was long and uneventful; by 3:35, Adam was on his way home.

Following dinner, Adam met up with Maggie in their special place, under the willow tree, like the previous evening. Maggie flipped through the pages of a textbook—this time, geography.

"Maggie, I was thinking. It's so nice of you to take the time to study with me, I want to help you in some way. I thought that I could come to the General Store after work and help out, if you'd like. I have time on Saturdays."

Adam was thinking there's no better place to be than with Maggie, even if it meant giving up his day off to work at the General Store.

"That would be wonderful, Adam. And we could certainly use your help there. Mr. Davis isn't doing too well, and it's hard for me to unload the merchandise sometimes, especially when Sister Agatha comes. She always stocks up for the orphanage, and she's had to load up her wagon by herself these past few Saturdays. I think she would be mighty grateful for a helping hand."

"Okay, then, I'd be happy to help you."

"Thanks, Adam. That would be great."

CHAPTER 4

THE ORPHANAGE

That Saturday, Adam rode his horse to the General Store and saw Maggie working at the counter.

"Hello, Maggie," Adam greeted her, trying to contain his excitement.

"Hello, Adam," Maggie replied, her cheeks blushing. She was thrilled to see him.

Mrs. Davis walked up from the back of the store. "Hello, Adam. It's so very good of you to come to help us."

"Hello, Mrs. Davis. When I heard your husband had been ill, I thought I could help you today with Sister Agatha's delivery. I am sorry to hear about Mr. Davis. I wish him a speedy recovery."

"Thank you, Adam. How kind of you. Sister Agatha always comes by at midday. We would be much obliged if you could help us load her wagon.

"You know, Adam, Sister Agatha is quite a woman," Mrs. Davis continued. "Five years ago, she came to this town from the East Coast, not knowing a soul and new to the Sisterhood. A few years later, when the Mother Superior passed away, she took the initiative to handle some of their special projects. One of the most important missions she completed was the opening of the orphanage.

"Over the last few years, she has taken so many children into the orphanage. I think there are over thirty now. Sister Agatha didn't want them to rely on charity alone, so they began to plant their own crops. Now they have a successful farm they maintain themselves, and they sell their crops in town to support themselves. She's thirty-five years old and more youthful than ever. And her children . . . why, they are better mannered than the Governor's own children!"

Adam soon discovered that Mrs. Davis loved to talk, and she always found kind things to say about everyone in town.

By noon, Sister Agatha, accompanied by Sister Mary, pulled up in front of the General Store. Maggie and Adam came outside to greet them.

Both Sisters were dressed in the long black habits of their order. The loose, flowing robes did not hide Sister Agatha's slim figure. Her pretty face was perfectly framed by the white band of the traditional headpieces they both wore, and her youthfulness was very apparent in contrast to Sister Mary, her matronly, much older companion.

"Good afternoon, Sisters," said Maggie.

"How are you, Maggie? Good to see you," Sister Agatha greeted her warmly.

"This is my friend, Adam," Maggie said. "He'll be helping you load up your wagon today."

Sister Agatha shook Adam's hand, and said, with a smile, "It's a pleasure to meet you, Adam. I appreciate your coming over to help us."

Sister Mary introduced herself to Adam and hurried off to do some other errands in town.

Maggie, Adam, and Sister Agatha entered the store, and Mrs. Davis greeted Sister Agatha.

"Hello, Sister Agatha. How are you? What'll it be today?" Mrs. Davis asked.

Agatha took out a list and handed it to Mrs. Davis. "We need just a few things today."

"Wonderful. Will you help me gather the purchases, Maggie?" Mrs. Davis asked.

"Of course," Maggie responded and walked over to her.

Sister Agatha said, "I must go over to the convent for a moment, but I'll be right back."

Maggie took the list and walked through each aisle, collecting the goods, and placing them in baskets, which Adam carried outside to the wagon. By the time Sister Agatha returned, the wagon was fully loaded.

Sister Agatha commented, "Mr. Davis used to help me carry the food into the orphanage. Then he'd bring back the baskets to the store. Would you two like to come and help us out today?" Turning to Adam, she added, "I'd love you to meet the other nuns and children."

"I would like that," Adam said, waiting for Maggie to say she'd join them.

But, instead he heard Maggie say, "I'm sorry, Sister Agatha, I have to go straight home today to finish up some chores. But thank you for inviting me."

Adam concealed his disappointment and waved goodbye to Maggie, as he and Agatha left the store.

"I'll see you on Monday, Adam," Maggie called out. "Have a nice time."

Adam retrieved his horse and rode alongside the nuns' wagon until they reached the orphanage.

The trip took a little over twenty minutes from the General Store, down past the Governor's mansion, and continuing to curve westward on Governor's Road, until the path forked in two—a dirt road and a cobblestone road.

They followed the dirt road another three miles south and entered the vast panorama of the hills. There, on the horizon, perched amidst the lush vegetation in the hills, was Sister Agatha's orphanage.

When they arrived, they were greeted by Mr. Loomis, an elderly widower who served as the live-in carpenter and general caretaker. He was in need of food, shelter, and companionship, and had moved in a year after his wife died. He was good to the Sisters; and he loved the children very much, especially since he had none of his own. Mr. Loomis' talents came in handy. His skills ranged from building furniture, to working the farm, to repairing anything that needed fixing. Over the years, he came to be a trusted member of the orphanage family.

The three of them walked through the archway to the main entrance, which had been beautifully hand-carved by Mr. Loomis. The building was constructed of thick planks of wood with lovely detailing.

As they stood in the parlor, and Adam looked around, he found it hard to believe it was just a modest orphanage. It was so clean and spacious.

To the left of the entranceway was a hall leading to a large room where the children slept. To the right was a hall leading to the living quarters for several of the sisters who took care of the children. Both hallways had entrances to the dining room directly in front of him.

The dining room was massive and also served as a play area. There was a huge rectangular table in the center and chairs all around. Chess sets and checkers, chalk and picture books, wood blocks, and dolls were stacked neatly around the room. The kitchen was situated beyond the dining room; it, too, connected to both the children's wing and the nuns' wing.

"The children are playing outside," Sister Agatha said. "Let's bring everything in, Adam, and then I'll introduce you."

Adam carried the baskets of groceries into the kitchen, emptied the contents, and placed the empty baskets into a large sack that was draped over his horse. Then he joined Sister Agatha outside.

"Good afternoon!" Sister Agatha called out to the children.

They all stopped playing and waved to Sister Agatha, shouting back, "Good afternoon, Sister Agatha!"

"Children, please say hello to our visitor, Adam, who has helped me bring our groceries from town."

"Hello, Adam." they responded.

Sister Agatha spoke softly to Adam as she told him about each child. They walked around the front yard while the children resumed playing.

"Clark is the eldest. He's fifteen years old and very strong and healthy. He's a big help around here. Russell is twelve and is also a fit young man, but he can be very outspoken. James is a sweet boy, about ten, and is the best listener of all. Steven is six—he's been very sad since losing his family in a tragic fire three months ago. But he's starting to feel better these days, and occasionally, we see him smiling.

"There's Elsa," Sister Agatha continued as they strolled. "She's a sweet girl who is almost seven, and she's the liveliest of the group. Selma is ten and the most outgoing, confident child. Janie is eight and is quiet and reserved, but she's the most obedient—a beautiful girl. And Rachel, with her lovely red hair, is five; she is charming but quiet."

Sister Agatha continued to tell Adam about each child and explained how they came to be at the orphanage. All had lost their parents through the hardships common to life at the time: to the dangerous voyages and diseases, to cold winters and fevers, to lumber and gunshot accidents, and so on.

"I look forward to spending time with all of them," Adam said to Agatha, as they walked back into the building.

Before he left, he briefly met the five other nuns who lived at the orphanage, and they all thanked him for his help.

Adam enjoyed his visit with Sister Agatha so much that he said he'd be happy to help her each week thereafter. She gratefully accepted his kind offer and invited Adam to come and bring Maggie for supper one evening. He thanked her for the invitation and headed home.

He rode his horse back to town, left the empty baskets behind the closed General Store, as instructed by Mrs. Davis, and then went home to join his family for supper.

The Starks family—all seven of them—sat around the table, passing around the platters of food. Adam was the oldest of three brothers and a sister. Jason was fourteen; Sam, twelve; and Jacob, seven; his sister, Cathy, was five. They all looked up to Adam, not only because he was the oldest, but because he was always watching out for them. Adam worried about them. He wondered if they were aware of the hardships the family was going through and the pressures their parents felt to make ends meet.

It was only through their tremendous efforts that James and Samantha Starks could provide for their family and put food on the table. And Adam's contribution now only made it a little easier.

James worked hard at the mines, forever hoping to impress Mr. Fitz enough to earn a raise. Samantha cooked, cleaned, and cared for the five children and was exhausted by the end of the day.

She sewed her family's clothing from whatever fabrics were cheapest at the General Store. She made sure they had one good Sunday outfit. Shoes were repaired and passed down from child to child. And they made do.

"How was your day at the store, Adam?" his father asked.

"Just fine, Pa. I met Sister Agatha today, and she's very nice. I offered to help them out at the orphanage on Saturdays."

"That's good of you, son," Adam's mother replied.

"Yes, it was nice to meet all the orphaned children today."

"Were any of the orphans my age?" asked Cathy.

"Yes, Cathy, and Jacob—there were boys and girls your age, too. There's a boy named Steven who is a year younger than you. You'd like him."

Adam continued to tell his family about the orphanage while they finished their meal.

CHAPTER 5

THE FALL

Three years passed. Adam worked with Jack and the crew every day mining for gold. Then, he would meet with Maggie on her free evenings to study whatever she had learned in school. Adam became a skilled miner who would be briefed on the day's work by the foreman and then sent off with a crew to dig. With Maggie's help, his education continued, and he felt good about how his life was going.

On one particular Friday evening, Adam and Maggie sat closer than usual on the grass under the willow tree. He closed the American History book they had been reading, and he kissed her on the cheek. Maggie blushed a bit, but it felt so natural to be close. They sat together hand-in-hand until their 8 p.m. curfew, watching a spectacular summer sunset beyond the horizon. Beauty and love filled their hearts and souls.

Adam continued to help Sister Agatha at the orphanage on Saturdays, and after spending so much time there, a very close bond of love and affection developed between Adam and the children.

Sister Agatha thought of Adam as one of her own and delighted in seeing him together with his beautiful girlfriend, Maggie.

Mr. and Mrs. Davis were thrilled to have Adam helping them, even after Mr. Davis had recovered. Mr. Davis was able to take more time off and worry less about the responsibilities of running the store.

On Adam's 18th birthday, he rushed home from the mine, bathed, shaved, and shot out the door like a bullet to see Maggie at the General Store. He was extremely excited about today. He had a special evening planned with Maggie, and he couldn't wait to see her.

Her eyes shined when she saw him. She was busy helping the neighborhood gossip, Miss Olson, get a sack of flour. Miss Olson had seen Adam come in, and she immediately strolled away to browse the aisles.

Adam found Maggie behind the counter, hugged her for a brief moment, and whispered to her, "When can you close tonight, Maggie? It's my birthday, you know."

"Of course, I know, silly."

Adam gave her a kiss.

She giggled and said "Miss Olson's in the store, Adam, and you know she sees and hears everything and talks to everyone in town."

"Yes, I know, Maggie," and he gave her another big kiss.

"Help me, and I can finish early," she responded. Adam nodded and went to find Miss Olson, who was in the far aisle. She pointed to the items she needed on the shelves, and Adam climbed the ladder from behind the counter to get them.

Just then, he heard two rowdy men enter the store, laughing and shouting vulgarities.

Adam stared out from the ladder and recognized the town's tough guys, Harry and Peter. They were also Mr. Fitz's bodyguards. They seemed to be drunk as they stumbled into the store.

"How can I help you?" Maggie asked, forcing a smile to hide her fear.

"Tobacco, sweetheart," said Harry.

Maggie turned around to grab a bag of tobacco. When she turned back to face Harry, he was now behind the counter and directly facing her, no more than a foot away.

Maggie screamed, but Peter reached his arm over the counter to cover her mouth. Harry grabbed Maggie and attempted to kiss her while she shoved him away. Tears rolled down Maggie's cheeks as she trembled.

Adam sprung off the ladder, pushed Peter aside, and dove onto Harry's back, forcing the two to collide onto the floor. Maggie fell back behind the counter. Adam struggled on the floor with Harry, punching him in the face and then rose to his feet to punch Peter in the stomach.

Harry grabbed Adam's foot while Peter punched him in the face, knocking Adam back down to the ground. Harry punched Adam again, and Peter jumped on top of him and landed another punch.

Then they abruptly released Adam, who was squirming in pain on the floor. They hopped over the counter laughing loudly and began to knock down some of the groceries from the shelves, before finally leaving.

Adam tried to get up, but the pain in his stomach was too great. Maggie rushed over to help him. His nose was bleeding, and he had a dark purple bruise on the right side of his face. She helped him to his feet, and they embraced.

From the corner of his eye, Adam saw Miss Olson emerging from one of the aisles, with none of her groceries, running out of the store.

Maggie helped Adam to a chair by the counter, and while he sat, she straightened up the mess. Then they closed up the store and left.

Maggie held Adam tightly, supporting his weight, as they walked outside together. They slowly traveled the distance to their quiet spot under the willow tree. She pulled a handkerchief from her bag and began to clean the blood around his face, kissing him softly. She couldn't hold back the tears that were welling up in her eyes, and they began to stream down her face.

"Some birthday celebration," Maggie said, trying to smile through her tears.

"Spread out the blanket, Maggie." Adam leaned against the tree trunk while Maggie set things up.

She laid out the blanket under the tree and set down the picnic basket she had prepared that morning. Then she helped Adam sit down, and he lay his head against the willow's enormous roots.

She opened the basket and took out the two sandwiches, keeping one for herself and giving the other to Adam.

Adam quickly sat up, looked at his sandwich, and with his eyes widened in panic, said, "Hey, wait a minute. I think that sandwich is mine, Maggie," and he quickly grabbed the sandwich from her hands and made the switch.

Maggie squinted at him, confused. "That's funny; they're both the same."

Adam took a bite of the sandwich and said, "Mmm . . . yes, this one's mine."

Maggie laughed and unwrapped her sandwich.

Right there, on top of her sandwich, in the center of the bread, lay a wooden ring. Maggie gasped and put her hand over her mouth. Adam took the ring from the bread and held it in front of her.

"I made it especially for you, Maggie. I put it in the sandwich when I got to the store." Adam's voice was trembling with excitement. "There's a carving inside the shank of the ring: 'A + M forever'."

Maggie looked at Adam, who was beaming with joy. She saw his beautiful—although battered—face, his goodness, his soul. She looked up at the stars to thank the heavens for sending her this beautiful man, who obviously loved her so completely.

"I already spoke to your father, Maggie. He said he would be happy to give me your hand in marriage . . . if that's what you want, of course. I love you, Maggie, and I want to be with you always. I promise to buy you a real gold ring as soon as I'm able, and I will take care of you and love you for all of our lives. Will you marry me?"

At that moment, Maggie thought she would explode with happiness. Her feelings overwhelmed her, and her eyes filled with tears again, but tears of a different kind.

"Everything will be okay, you know, Maggie. I promise you."

Maggie threw her arms around Adam and responded, "I know we'll be happy, Adam, and I love you very much. Yes, I will marry you."

They hugged tightly and remained in each other's arms for the rest of the evening.

When Adam got home that night, his parents were shocked to see his battered face. He immediately dismissed his bruises as unimportant and told his parents the exciting news. They all hugged and congratulated him.

The following day, Adam awoke with back and stomach pain, and a large red welt around his right eye. He got on his horse feeling the pain but ignored it as he rode to the mines, excited and smiling all the way, thinking about Maggie. He arrived just in time to see Jack about to descend on the pulley to their dig site.

"Good morning, Jack," Adam called out.

"Hello son. Hey, what in the world happened to you?" Jack asked. "You look terrible."

"Yeah, it's nothing. I'm fine, Jack. I had a bit of a rough night with a sweet ending. Maggie and I are to be married. I proposed to her and she accepted! I don't think there's a man in the world as happy as me today."

"Well, that's wonderful. Congratulations, Adam." Jack went over and hugged him.

As the two descended underground on the pulley, Jack explained the day's work. "I have a difficult assignment for you today, Adam. There's a new dig site that we need to open up. It's a very narrow space; almost impossible for most of the men to get into, but you're small enough to fit and strong enough to clear the rock from around you to make room to work. There's no one else on the team that can do it.

"And, Adam, I have a very good feeling about this spot. Mr. Fitz has finally said that he'll be giving big bonuses to the men who make the next major discovery, and this could be it."

Jack led Adam down through the main opening of the mine which took several minutes, until they came to a network of tunnels. The tunnel farthest right had the smallest entrance. Jack dropped to his knees and pressed his elbows to the ground, crawling with Adam down the dark, chilly passageway for about fifty feet, until they came to the part of the tunnel that narrowed even more.

"Here's where you go on your own, Adam. Ten more feet, and you'll see the area."

Adam had to use all his strength to squeeze into the small space where he was supposed to dig. He had a very limited range of motion, and his aching body from yesterday's beating made it even worse. He wondered how he could even possibly begin. But he did.

"Are you going to be okay here, Adam? I need to get back to the crew," Jack yelled from the other side of the narrow tunnel.

"Sure, Jack. I'm fine."

Jack crawled out through the tunnel, and Adam was alone now. He might have felt frightened on an ordinary day, but this was certainly no ordinary day.

He kept thinking about last night's events—Maggie had said yes! He thought about their future. They had been together since the first day they spoke at the General Store three years ago, but things were much different now. They were older now and knew each other so well. They were meant to be together, and now they'd be able to start a family soon.

Adam had been saving up a small portion of his salary, ever since he made the decision to propose to Maggie. He was almost ready to put some money down on a lovely piece of property on the outskirts of Goldstone. He would be able to build them a home—nothing too big, but a real home of their own.

As Adam worked, he thought of all this, and it made him labor faster and harder. He wanted to be able to take care of Maggie, and the bonus he would receive for finding gold in this tunnel would be a huge help in paying for the wedding and starting their lives together.

Adam quickly cleared enough space around him to be able to swing his arms freely, and then he worked like a machine. He slammed his pickaxe into the hard rock in front of him over and over again, each blow coming harder and harder and then picking up the pace—faster and faster, with even more force than the last.

His heart was beating hard and fast, almost in rhythm with the blows of his axe. His entire body was drenched in sweat—more and more kept pouring out of his forehead and armpits.

His muscles started to burn with the kind of pain that a champion fighter must feel when he's reached his limit and is hoping for the bell.

But he wouldn't stop. The pain meant that he was working toward a better life with Maggie. He would find the gold and make the bonus money for Maggie. He wanted her to have everything.

After clearing the ground around him, he could finally stand up and stretch comfortably. He started to hammer in the wooden studs to reinforce the walls around him when all of a sudden, the ground beneath him began to rumble. It felt like the rumbling of an earthquake. Within seconds, the ground supporting him gave way. He started falling through a crevice that opened up as the ground split beneath him.

Luckily, one foot caught on the ledge and kept him above the surface. The other foot was hanging loose over a big opening that was now at least thirty feet deep.

Finally, the trembling stopped, and all was quiet. It took him a moment to understand what had happened. While still in shock, he saw a gleaming wall of golden rock through the opening below.

He tried to lift himself up and suddenly felt an extremely sharp pain in his upper leg.

He looked down and saw that a sharp, thick shard of gold-rippled rock had pierced through his right thigh from back to front. It was pinning him against the wall and held him from falling; he couldn't move. The trauma of the accident heightened his senses in a strange way. He wasn't panicked. In fact, he felt more alert and his senses sharpened.

He listened closely but heard nothing, other than the faint sound of water flowing down a rock formation off in the distance. He didn't hear any sounds of rescue, which may have meant no one heard his fall. Since no one had come to check on him all morning, the thought crossed his mind that the crew may have been working on a dig site far away. He was trapped and all alone. He tried calling out for help, but there was no one around to hear him.

It was midday, and Adam thought that the shift would be over in a couple of hours. They would surely expect him on the pick-up wagon, and when he wasn't there, they would come down and find him.

The pain was increasing, and after some initial tingling, he lost the feeling in his wounded leg entirely. He started to feel light-headed but forced himself to remain focused. He again concentrated on Maggie and the wonderful future they would share. He would survive this and see her beautiful face again. And he thought of his family and how much he loved them. He had to hang on, but for how long? He just wished they would find him quickly.

On the other side of the mines, everyone was busy with explosives. They blasted a hole in the mountain to start digging a new tunnel. And promptly at 3:30, at the end of their shift, everyone went home and forgot about Adam.

When Adam wasn't home by 4, James Starks assumed his son had gone to visit Maggie at the General

Store. When he wasn't home by 6, James thought that maybe they were studying or had taken a stroll in town. By 9 p.m., James was very concerned. Adam never came home after 9; he would always tell his family where he was going to be if he planned to be home late.

James went over to Maggie's house to look for Adam. Maggie and her parents were about to turn in and were surprised to see Mr. Starks.

Maggie said that she hadn't seen Adam that night—they had no plans to meet.

"Is everything okay?" she asked with concern.

"I don't know," he responded. "I'm suspecting that something might have gone wrong at the mines, or maybe something happened to him on his way home. I'm on my way to see the foreman. Try not to worry, and get some sleep. I'll see you in the morning."

Mr. Starks got back on his horse and rode to Jack's house. The foreman was surprised to see him and could tell that something was wrong.

When James told Jack that Adam had not come home, Jack thought for a moment and said, "I was working on another mine today, blasting a new area to dig. I didn't make it back before 4, so I just assumed that Adam and the others had made it back on the cart at 3:30. Are you telling me he didn't make it back?"

" I don't think he did, Jack."

"We should go back to the mines. I set him up in a tough shaft today, but he was handling it beautifully, James. Let's go, I'll take you over to his dig site."

The two men rode their horses to the mines. The sky was dark and the air, cool. The darkness gave the landscape a surreal feeling. The two miners were rarely there past sunset, and the area was isolated. Trying to shake off the feeling of dread, they lowered themselves on the pulley and went underground.

They took the cart, then hiked to the tunnel, and crawled through the shaft. Neither man spoke a word.

As they entered the narrow passageway, both men dropped to their knees and looked down. What they saw was an enormous hole that now occupied the area. There was only a narrow ledge to stand on surrounding it. Jack and James stood in disbelief.

Adam heard something and yelled, "HELLO, IS SOMEONE UP THERE?"

James got down on his knees on the damp ground and lowered his lantern into the pit. To his astonishment, he saw Adam clinging to the cliff wall, ten feet below.

"Adam! We're here, Son," his father called out. "How are you doing?"

"There's a rock stuck in me, Pa," he yelled back. "It's lodged in my thigh. I . . . I can't move."

James turned to face Jack, who said, "He's been down there for hours, James. Let's go get some help."

As they got down on their knees to crawl out of the tunnel, James called out, "We'll be back, Son. Stay strong."

Jack rubbed his eyes as they hurried to retrace their steps. Both men were visibly shaken; the fear they felt showed in their faces.

Adam breathed a deep sigh of relief. He allowed himself to relax a bit, knowing he was found and would be freed shortly. He closed his eyes.

By midnight, Jack and James returned with a crew of men, ropes, and cutting equipment. They had to clear some large rock formations to enlarge the passageway to get to Adam. They formed a line as one man filled a bucket and passed it along to the next in line until it was dumped above ground. They worked to dig out a ledge on which to support the men who would pull Adam up. The heat was stifling and the work was brutal. Each miner was covered in sweat and, as the hours passed, they worked to the brink of exhaustion.

As the rescue operation was underway, a crowd of onlookers gathered. Adam's mother and siblings had been waiting since daybreak, along with Maggie and her parents. Mr. and Mrs. Davis didn't open the store that morning, as they waited with the other townspeople at the mine for Adam to be pulled to safety.

Down below, Adam faded in and out of consciousness; he had lost so much blood. The crew continued to work, and by noon, they had finally cleared enough space to be able to proceed down with ropes to tie him up for support. As they pulled him off the wall, Adam passed out.

They raised him up towards the tunnel, as blood continued to drip from his wound. After bandaging his leg to stop the bleeding, Adam was carried out through the tunnel, into the cart, and out of the mine. He was then rushed to the nearest doctor.

Adam spent the rest of the day unconscious in a bed at the doctor's home. The next day, his wounded leg had gotten worse. Several doctors from neighboring towns came to see him, and all agreed that the leg must be amputated in order for him to survive.

But Adam's father refused to let his son lose his leg. James carried Adam out to the wagon, and they rode west toward Professor Morgansteen's place. They reached the secluded shack about a mile outside of town and knocked on the door.

CHAPTER 6

PROFESSOR MORGANSTEEN

Professor Morgansteen was not welcome in town. He had lost his medical license many years earlier, and only a few people who knew him from earlier days still trusted him and saw him secretly.

It had not always been this way. He was a good doctor. In fact, he had helped Adam's mother deliver her baby girl. There were dire complications during labor, and both had nearly died. Thanks to Professor Morgansteen, the child and mother survived. James Starks and his family trusted him completely.

For the first half of his life, the Professor had followed a path that was quite fortunate and led to great success.

He grew up in California but was educated in the East, attending a prominent university and then earning a medical degree there. After completing his education, the head of the university urged him to stay on to teach there.

Understanding the need for advanced medical training of future students, he agreed. Within two years, he became the head of the medical department of the school and was credited with developing great advancements in the program there.

But the Professor yearned to use his knowledge to help the sick. Three years later, he returned to California to practice medicine, bringing his beautiful fiancée, Clara, along with him.

Soon they married and settled into a new home. Professor Morgansteen started a medical practice in Goldstone with a partner, Dr. Richmond. The Professor was a happy, well respected man with a good life.

Then, suddenly, disaster struck. His wife, Clara, became seriously ill, and nobody, not even the Professor, could diagnose the illness. She was weak with a high fever and could not get out of bed.

The Professor desperately sought council with the most renowned doctors across the country and researched all the available medical journals to find a cure. But he couldn't save her; Clara was dead within a month. The man was never the same after that.

Professor Morgansteen realized that conventional treatments were not enough. In order to save lives, he needed to look at science in more unconventional ways to treat his patients.

As time went on, he spent less and less time seeing patients, and more and more time in a makeshift laboratory in the back room of his home. His partner, who had once felt privileged to be working with the Professor, broke away to start a practice on his own.

Morgansteen was now alone and had no real source of income. He also had few needs now that his beloved Clara was gone. So he stayed in his secluded shack to work on his research.

The Professor barely noticed the sun rising or setting for the next seven years. His life was his research, his microscope, and lab equipment. His once robust body became frail. He grew a long beard, and his hair turned gray. He only left his home to get food and other necessities.

Through his trips to the General Store, he developed a friendship with Maggie, and later, with Adam, too. Maggie and Adam would deliver special items when shipments arrived and just generally checked in on him.

The Professor spent almost all of his time on his research. He gathered leaves and berries in the surrounding woods and crushed them with a mortar and pestle. Then he fed the mixtures to various animals to treat their illnesses and to examine the effects. The yard behind his house was practically a zoo, filled with animals that he cared for and healed with his medicines.

It was hard for most people to understand the Professor. Many of them said that he had never gotten over the death of his wife—that he'd completely lost his mind; others speculated that he might be doing some unsavory medical research. The vast majority of the population saw the Professor as a deranged madman and kept their distance. Professor Morgansteen was unfazed by the townspeoples' talk. In fact, due to his lifestyle, he was almost completely unaware of it.

Finally, after a dreadfully long and dark period during which he thought he might never make progress, he began to see some positive results on the animals.

He found ways to make wounds heal faster than ever before. He could make sick creatures well again when they seemed doomed to death. Some of these miraculous cures were witnessed by workers in the surrounding woods, and word began to spread that the Professor was curing sick animals.

One day, the Professor showed Adam and Maggie a new experimental remedy to heal bones and skin remarkably fast. Right before their eyes, he cured a lame horse that had been injured while plowing a neighbor's field.

The horse's leg had been completely broken and ordinarily would have been put out of it's misery immediately with a single bullet to the head. But the farmer had heard of the Professor and his magical brew. With one dose, the horse was up and running again.

There were many illnesses in town, and many desperate people who were in need of more advanced treatments than were generally available. And so they began to seek treatment from the good Professor once more—a few people at first, but then in increasing numbers.

They waited in line to see the Professor, and he was able to help many of them—but not all. He felt that even though he had come so far, he still needed to continue his research.

He treated patients during the day and on an emergency basis, but continued his research, working through the nights on his various potions and ointments, testing on animals and then on a human subject—himself.

He injected himself with the cholera bacteria and began to suffer severe symptoms. When his fever reached 102 degrees, he swallowed his special medicine and immediately felt the effects. His fever subsided, and he realized he had cured himself. The Professor was thrilled with the progress.

He went back to the lab and continued his work, concentrating on combining and re-combining substances, experimenting on the animals and himself, and evaluating the results.

Then, one night, something magical happened. As he was mixing his latest formula, he suddenly felt a divine presence enveloping him. As the green liquid bubbled in a glass beaker, it seemed as if all the powers of the universe were at one within him. He felt a clarity, a certainty, and then, tremendous excitement.

The realization that he had achieved his mission sent chills down his spine. And just at that moment, the sky rumbled with thunder—applause from the heavens!

At last, Professor Morgansteen knew that he had his curing potion.

He soaked swabs with infectious bacteria of incurable disease cells and touched them to his tongue. Then he took a knife and made a deep incision on his left forearm and infected that with a fatal viral bacteria.

After he started to feel the symptoms of the diseases, he swallowed some of the special combination of leaves, herbs, berries, tree bark, and chemicals that made up the potion. He also spread an ointment on his wounded arm made from the same ingredients.

Without having any confirmation of his success, but at the same time absolutely sure of it, the Professor collapsed backwards into bed and fell asleep. He slept for twenty-four hours, and when he woke up—though he was extremely hungry and thirsty—his wound had healed completely, and he no longer had symptoms of any of the deadly diseases.

Perhaps he would have to make some modifications here and there, but the Professor was positive that he had finally succeeded and could go on with his life's mission. His magical solution was complete.

He took a deep breath. Now he could help others the way he always wanted to.

The Professor did not have to wait long to be of service. When illness takes over and there is no hope, people who need a miracle will go anywhere to find it.

Mr. Riley, the blacksmith, was at death's door when he decided to see the Professor as a last resort. When the Professor cured him, news spread quickly through the town. Professor Morgansteen offered a miracle.

Patients started to line up at his door again, with all sorts of serious ailments, and the good Professor cured them.

One day, he was awakened in the dark early morning hours by loud knocking on the door of his shack. When he opened it, he was greeted by a tall, well dressed man in a suit. "I am a representative of Governor Tannin. He needs your help right away. It's an emergency."

"Bring the patient inside," the Professor replied.

"It's the Governor's daughter, Sir, and he asks that you treat her at his home. I'm here to take you to the Governor's mansion."

The Professor grabbed his bag and was whisked into the waiting carriage.

Within a few minutes, they arrived at the Governor's mansion. The Professor was surprised by the enormous wealth displayed in the furnishings. The Governor seemed to live like a king.

The Professor fleetingly wondered where all of the Governor's wealth had come from, but he didn't have time to finish his thoughts before he was ushered into the Governor's office.

He sat down on a fine leather chair, in front of a hand-carved oak table, opposite Governor Tannin. The room had dark wood paneling and heavy red velvet curtains framing large fancy windows. The sun was just rising, and the early morning light poured in and cast a glow on the Governor's pudgy face.

"Professor Morgansteen," said Tannin, "they say you're the best doctor in town, even though I hear your methods are a bit, shall we say . . . unorthodox.

"You see, Sir, my daughter, Prudence, is suffering from a terrible illness. She's running a very high fever—coughing and vomiting, delirious all the time. All of the doctors I've spoken to say there's nothing to be done. I've heard you perform miracles, and I don't really care about your methods, Professor, just please save my daughter."

The Professor nodded his head. "And," the Governor added, "if you do a good job, you will be handsomely compensated."

"Oh, there's no need for that, Governor," Professor Morgansteen replied. "My rates are always the same."

The Governor was taken aback for a moment as he thought about the Professor's attitude. The nerve of that guy, the Governor concluded to himself. Who the hell did he think he was anyway?

Jeffrey Tannin believed everyone had a price, and if a man said he didn't, well then, he was just being arrogant. He decided immediately that he didn't like the Professor but thought if he was able to save Prudence, well, that was all he wanted.

The two men walked across the hall to the girl's bedroom, where she lay flushed with fever, damp with sweat, and extremely ill. Professor Morgansteen examined the patient, took her temperature, and drew some blood samples.

"I'm going to give Prudence a shot," the Professor said to the Governor. The twelve-year-old girl shuddered, apparently hearing the mention of a needle.

"Don't worry," the Professor said to his patient, "it won't hurt a bit." He injected her with a needle filled with the glowing green fluid. "This cure will work," the Professor said, "but," he looked directly at the Governor as he continued, "it is absolutely imperative that you do not allow your daughter to have anything to eat or drink for at least thirty-six hours. Just have her stay in bed and rest. The medicine will increase her appetite and parch her thirst significantly, but she must not eat or drink anything until tomorrow night. If you don't follow these directions, it could have severe consequences. Do you understand?"

The Governor nodded. "That won't be a problem."

Professor Morgansteen left, feeling confident that the girl would pull through.

The Governor was preparing to have his big annual meeting with the town's business leaders the following day. Many rich and powerful men—and a few women— were to be in attendance, including Mr. Fitz.

Prudence slept all day and all night. When she awoke the next morning, she cried that she was hungry and thirsty, but her father ignored her—he knew he couldn't give her anything until later that evening.

The Governor needed to have his mind clear for the meeting and decided the best way to deal with his daughter was to lock her up in her room. He thought she'd be fine alone—she was supposed to rest anyway. So after checking up on her mid-morning, he locked the door on his way out.

Not long after her father left the room, Prudence gathered all her strength and embarked on a mission to find some food. She had regained some of her stamina, but she was so hungry and thirsty. She cautiously climbed out the window to the balcony and onto the ground below. Then she walked through an opened window to the kitchen.

She was relieved to see that nobody was there. Her father's meeting had started, and while the staff was attending to the guests, she made her way to the cookie jar and devoured several sugar cookies. She then consumed some of the stew the cook had prepared for the luncheon, and she washed it down with a glass of milk. When her hunger and thirst had been satisfied, she retraced her steps to the bedroom and drifted off to sleep.

Later that day, when the Governor had completed his meeting, he retired to his room and sent a member of his office staff to check on his daughter. The worker ran back to the Governor in a panic, saying, "Sir, something's wrong. Come quick."

The Governor's face dropped as he entered her room. There she lay, pale as snow, lifeless—dead. The Governor was mortified. "GET ME THE PROFESSOR," he shouted. "Oh my poor baby," he cried. "What has that madman done to you?"

The Governor's aide fetched the Professor from his home and brought him into the Governor's parlor.

"My daughter is gone, Professor, and it's all your fault." The Professor examined the girl and realized that she had eaten.

When he told the Governor that this was the case, the Governor said, "That's a lie! It's not possible. She was locked in her room the whole time."

The Governor pleaded with the Professor, "Do something."

The Professor responded, "I can help the sick, Sir, but I cannot bring back the dead. I'm terribly sorry, Governor."

This comment enraged the Governor, and he threw the Professor out of the mansion.

As soon as the Professor left, the Governor's aide whispered into the Governor's ear that, in fact, the cook had mentioned to him that some stew was missing from the kitchen, and an empty glass of milk was found on the kitchen table.

"Perhaps Prudence got out somehow and made it to the kitchen," the aide said.

But the Governor hushed him immediately and said, "Not a word to anyone about this. It's that madman's fault my daughter's gone."

The next day, the Governor addressed the townspeople in the Square: "Yesterday, in my most desperate hour, I turned to Professor Morgansteen to help cure my daughter of her illness. She just needed conventional treatment. But the Professor assured me that he had a new way of doing things, a 'quick fix' that would have my daughter free of her ills. I was a bit apprehensive about it, but he told me that it was absolutely safe. So I let him give it to her. I wish I had never listened to that madman!" he shouted, his face turning red.

He pointed to Professor Morgansteen in the crowd and screamed, "THAT MAN'S POISON KILLED MY DAUGHTER! I can never get her back!" He paused for a moment to compose himself and then continued. "But I can make sure that nobody else ever gets treatment from this quack.

"Morgansteen, I hereby strip you of your medical license! It will now be against the law for any of you to go to Morgansteen for medical treatment."

He continued as he stared at the Professor, "And you should consider yourself lucky not to be charged with murder. For shame! For shame!"

A gasp rose from the crowd, and everyone turned toward the Professor. Many of the townspeople started to mumble horrible things about him, and some of them threw nasty glances in his direction. He was being pushed out of the crowd by the angry bystanders and was forced to leave and retreat to his shack.

Professor Morgansteen was chased into isolation that day and had to practice medicine in secret. He lost contact with most of the townspeople who had lost trust in him anyway. But Maggie and Adam and their families always kept in friendly contact with him and trusted him.

Since the Professor had no family of his own, he often celebrated the holidays with Maggie, Adam, and their families. Quite often, Adam and Maggie would come by to visit the Professor. They would play with his animals and watch his experiments. Maggie would cook and clean for the Professor, and he appreciated it. They brought some much needed joy into his life.

Adam enjoyed helping the Professor with his research and was like an assistant to him. He found that he had a talent for chemistry and wondered if he could ever go on to become a scientist or maybe a doctor himself. As time passed, their friendship grew, and the Professor became part of the family.

So now, there stood James Starks at the Professor's door, holding his unconscious son in his arms, drenched with sweat and trembling with fear. This was it, his son's last hope to live a normal life. He took a deep breath and knocked on the door. The Professor opened it and, with one look at Adam, said, "Get him over to the table."

James put Adam down on the table, and Professor Morgansteen immediately cleaned the wound, took some blood samples, and examined the leg closely. After he returned from his lab in the back of the shack, he had a concerned expression.

"James," he said, "your son's leg is in bad shape. It's really mangled. And I see that a significant amount of gold has entered his bloodstream. That's serious. It could be poisonous."

Mr. Starks' eyes started to well up with tears. He was afraid that his son might never be able to work in the gold mines again; that this big, strong young man would be rendered a cripple.

"There is one option, James," Professor Morgansteen continued, trying to console him, "I do have a medicine that I believe can save the leg and make it possible for Adam to walk again, but it's just out of the testing phase. It could be extremely risky for him, especially when the drug combines with the gold in his bloodstream.

"I'm just not sure how it will mix, James, and it could turn out to be lethal. We may be better off just amputating the leg. You know, it is possible for someone to live a happy, productive life with only one . . . "

"No," James interrupted, "that is not an option. My son cannot lose that leg. How will he make a living? He's planning to be married and start a family. Please, Professor, do whatever you can for my boy."

"Are you sure?" asked Professor Morgansteen, looking James directly in the eyes.

Mr. Starks nodded.

"Okay," said the Professor. "Let's get on with it."

The Professor reached into an icebox and pulled out a vial of a glowing blue liquid, and another filled with a thick, mud-colored paste. "The timing of this procedure is crucial," he said. "Wipe Adam's leg clean with this cloth and antiseptic." James did as the Professor instructed.

Then, Professor Morgansteen took a syringe and put it into the vial with the brownish paste, filling it halfway. He took a deep breath as he quickly filled the remainder of the hypodermic with the glowing blue fluid.

As soon as the chemicals combined, the liquid started to bubble like rapidly boiling water. With the vaccine still bubbling, the doctor injected the needle into Adam's leg. The Professor exhaled and wiped the sweat from his own forehead. "Now," he said, "all we can do is wait and hope for the best."

James and the Professor sat vigil, while Adam lay hooked up with tubes. They continuously monitored his vital signs. No visitors were allowed in; they wanted to keep germs to a minimum.

As the hours progressed, the Professor and James witnessed the miraculous healing of Adam's leg. After three days, it had healed so well that it would be impossible for any stranger to know that it had ever been injured at all, except for some discoloration where the gold shard had pierced his leg.

Adam awoke on the third day. He reached down to touch his leg. "My leg," he said in amazement. "It's healed! I can't believe it!"

"We injected you with a special medication," the Professor explained, "and it's healed you, Adam. You should be perfectly able to walk and work now without any limitations—just as you did before the fall."

Adam hopped off the table and tested the strength of his leg, balancing on his right leg alone for a few moments and jogging from one end of the room to the other. He was amazed to find that he felt no pain at all.

"That's incredible, Professor," he said.

"Yes, it is, Adam" said the Professor, "but I must warn you of something." He paused. "Even though your leg has healed, there is still a significant amount of poisonous gold in your bloodstream. It is impossible to predict what effects it might have.

"And, as you can see, the skin around the wound on both the front and back of your leg is discolored. I can't explain the golden hue, but it must be that some remnants of the gold that entered your system were absorbed through your leg muscles."

This information would have disturbed most people, but Adam was overjoyed at having his leg back, so he paid no attention to the Professor's concerns. The discoloration didn't bother him at all.

After a week of rest, and to everyone's amazement, Adam returned to work at the mines. Jack's crew had begun mining the gold that Adam had discovered.

Adam's story turned out to be good publicity for Goldstone Mines. The Professor's reputation was restored to legendary status. And life went back to normal in the town of Goldstone.

CHAPTER 7

THE INDIANS

At home, the two families eagerly began making wedding preparations. With Sister Agatha's blessing and encouragement, Maggie and Adam agreed to have the marriage ceremony at the orphanage.

Three days prior to their marriage, Maggie accompanied Adam to the orphanage to make final arrangements. Sister Agatha greeted them and led them into the dining hall, which was being set up with white tablecloths, seat cushions on all the chairs, candles, and ornaments. The huge wooden table in the dining room was covered with festive decorations as well, and the chairs had been arranged so that everyone would have a proper seat.

After discussing all the details, Sister Agatha and Maggie went out to the fields, joining some of the children who were picking vegetables. The nuns were in the kitchen preparing dinner and setting aside the best silverware for the upcoming ceremony. A few of the children were playing in the front yard.

Adam was working with Mr. Loomis to build a platform for the ceremony that would be placed at the far end of the dining room.

While Mr. Loomis went to town to pick up some supplies, Adam was busy transferring lumber from the large shed about a hundred feet to the side of the main building. It stored a variety of tools, seeds, farming equipment, and kerosene.

Adam took his horse and buggy over to the shed to haul the wood to the platform area. He opened the squeaky wooden door and looked inside for the lumber. Although there were a few small windows, it was dark inside the large room, so Adam left the door open a crack and began to search for a lantern. He found one alongside the back wall with a box of matches beside it. Adam lit the lantern and carried it across the storage room, where he saw the pile of boards.

Just at that moment, he heard a commotion outside in the front yard of the main building.

He snuffed out the lantern's flame, dropped to the ground instinctively, and crawled his way to the shed door. He heard some yelling and the shuffling of hooves. Adam peered through the small opening of the door and saw a gang of hoodlums approaching the front of the orphanage.

Meanwhile, the children who had been playing in the front yard saw the men approaching and came running into the orphanage. Clark, the oldest boy, was the last one in. He closed the door and quickly barricaded it with wooden slats.

"What's that shouting? Who's there?" asked one of the Sisters, as they came running in from the kitchen.

"I know who it is," mumbled Sister Mary, as she peered through the window. "It's Pedro Gorticcio," she said—she paused to take a deep breath—"the most wanted man in the country."

Pedro Gorticcio and his gang were known to be ruthless and unmerciful murderers who took pride in leaving no survivors behind in robberies across the country, not even sparing the women or children. Sister Mary had seen his face on a 'Wanted Dead or Alive' poster in town, along with some of his gang members.

The Sisters hurried the children through the hallway to their bedroom in the back and tried their best to comfort them.

Gorticcio's men used a tree trunk as a battering ram and smashed through the doors of the orphanage. The gang always carried this particular tree trunk with them to use for break-ins. It was custom-made with a pointed iron end-cap; on the sides of the trunk were a row of metal handles. Five men held on to each side as they rammed through the orphanage door.

Once inside, they threw the tree trunk on the dining room table, loudly smashing it to pieces. A few of the men went to the back bedroom and brought the nuns and children out to the front yard.

Sister Agatha and Maggie came running in from the fields with the rest of the children. They clung to each other as they stood in front of Pedro Gorticcio, who sat proudly on his horse.

Adam had been watching the commotion from the shed. He hurried to his horse, carefully detached the wagon, and saddled up as fast as he could.

The leader of the gang was a short, stout, mean-looking man with a moustache, wearing a sombrero hat. "I am Pedro Gorticcio. I journey to you from my home in Mexico. Now, here, near Goldstone, I come with my most loyal compatriots. We need food and rest. You must give us your hospitality."

No one spoke—they were too frightened to respond—but some of the younger children started crying, and Gorticcio screamed, "SHUT UP. I WANT SILENCE!"

At this point, Sister Agatha stepped forward and said, "You must not yell at the children. We will give you what you ask for, and then you will be on your way."

Gorticcio pulled out his gun and pointed it at Sister Agatha. She didn't flinch. Gorticcio laughed. "I give the orders here, Sister."

At that moment, Gorticcio caught a glimpse of Adam riding his horse out beyond the shed.

"Aha!" he said to his men. "There's someone getting away!"

Gorticcio and three of his men turned around and shot in Adam's direction. Maggie shuttered with fear.

He was a great distance away, but when their guns went off, Gorticcio cheered in Spanish as they watched Adam fall off his horse and into the grass. He smiled and said to the group, “That’s what happens to anyone who tries to run away.” The nuns closed their eyes and made the sign of the cross.

“NOW,” Gorticcio demanded, “EVERYONE GET INSIDE!”

Adam had been hit in the left shoulder. He fell from the saddle, but his left foot got stuck in the strap, and he managed to hang on. He commanded his horse to proceed and was slowly dragged out of sight into the woods. He then stopped his horse, untangled his foot from the strap, and slowly stood up. He reached over to feel his wound. The bullet had gone right through his left arm near the shoulder, and it was bleeding heavily. Adam took a handkerchief from his pocket and tied it tightly around the arm. Then he climbed back onto his horse and rode off to see the Tommahoe Indian tribe.

Years earlier, the President of the United States issued The Indian Removal Act, evicting thousands of Native Americans from their land, forcing them to establish new settlements elsewhere.

North Star was a young Tommahoe warrior when his tribe was told to leave their land in Arizona as part of the Act.

The Tommahoe tribe was rebellious and many refused to obey and fought the new settlers. But North Star was a peaceful man. He was against warfare and decided that it would be best to move west. Others shared his belief. He assumed a position of leadership, becoming Chief of the new tribe that headed to California.

They set off on horseback and on foot, suffering many hardships along the long journey—disease, ambush attacks, extreme exertion, starvation, and death on their way to their new settlement.

By the time Chief North Star had reached California, his tribe had dwindled from twenty-five hundred to thirteen hundred members. They settled on a majestic mountain on the outskirts of town that they named Mount Dove. The wildlife was abundant, and the soil was rich for crops.

At the base of the mountain was a crystal clear river known as Valley Creek, surrounding Mount Dove in the shape of a crescent moon. A cascading waterfall ran down the eastern slopes; dense forest covered the rest of the mountain.

After making their new home on Mount Dove, the tribe was attacked and again suffered many casualties.

Sister Agatha was aware of the Tommahoe's history and saddened by it. She was the first to come to their aide. She tended to the wounded warriors and took the most severe casualties to the orphanage for recuperation.

Chief North Star's son, Wildwind, was one of the warriors with the worst injuries. He was saved by Sister Agatha, and since then, the friendship between the tribe and the orphanage was strong.

They often visited and exchanged gifts. The nuns sent the tribe fruit and vegetables grown at the orphanage, and the Chief sent buffalo meat and deer skins in return.

Maggie and Adam visited the tribe on several occasions delivering food, and they were invited many times to tribal ceremonies and celebrations. They had become good friends with the Chief's youngest daughter, Nema, and her husband, Timo; they were all about the same age.

Together they would ride their horses through the canyons of Mount Dove. Timo and Adam would fish and hunt together, while Nema and Maggie spent time at the Indian campsite. Nema taught Maggie how to weave beautiful baskets to sell at the General Store.

Timo showed Adam the concealed tunnels and trails the tribe had dug out behind the waterfall. The Tommahoes knew an escape route was needed in case of future attacks and created this secret passageway. Adam was the only person outside the tribe to be entrusted with this secret.

They were all very close friends. Adam trusted the Chief and his tribe completely and knew they would help.

The day Gorticcio and his gang attacked the orphanage, Adam traveled five miles to reach the river of Valley Creek at the base of Mount Dove.

As his horse passed over the crushed pebbles and rocks of the shallow part of the river, Adam knew that an Indian scout would report his arrival. The speed of his horse would signal the urgency. He pulled the reigns hard and embarked on the steep uphill journey to Mount Dove.

As Adam made his way to the summit, the signal was sent up through a series of scouts, and he could see Chief North Star was there to meet him—his long, flowing pure white hair, his large, muscular 6' 4" frame. As he got closer, he could also see the Chief's friendly, weathered face, showing concern.

"Chief, there's been an attack on the orphanage. Maggie's inside with all of the nuns and children. It's Pedro Gorticcio's gang."

The Chief took one look at Adam's arm and sent for the tribe's medicine woman. She examined the wound, applied some disinfecting ointment, and bandaged it up. A moment later, and without hesitation, Adam and the Chief—along with a hundred Tommahoe warriors—left on horseback.

Back at the orphanage, Gorticcio was terrorizing his captives. He instructed his men to tie up Sister Agatha and the other six nuns with rope and have them sit on the floor in the far left corner of the dining room. The children were told to sit in the opposite corner. He told Maggie to remain standing in the center of the room.

Gorticcio then motioned to his men to go through the rooms and look for valuables. As they ransacked the place, Gorticcio paced up and down the dining room, kicking pieces of the broken table on the floor as he walked.

He was mumbling to himself at first, but then he walked over to Maggie and yelled in her face, "GET ME FOOD!" And Maggie, never more frightened in her life, ran off to the kitchen.

The men returned to the dining room with a few silver crosses, cups, candle holders, and silverware, obviously disappointed in their limited bounty. Gorticcio inspected a couple of items and threw them across the room, nearly hitting the children. Enraged, he turned to Sister Agatha and yelled, "WHERE'S ALL THE MONEY?"

She responded, "We have no money here."

"WE'LL SEE ABOUT THAT!" Gorticcio screamed back at her.

At that moment, Maggie came running in with a large platter of meats, rice, and corn. She abruptly stopped about five feet in front of the men, fearing to get any closer to the madman.

One of the gang members pulled up a chair and took the platter from Maggie, placing it on the chair in front of Gorticcio. Maggie just stood there, frozen with fear. Gorticcio grabbed a piece of meat with his hands and savagely shoved it into his mouth. He grabbed an ear of corn with the other hand and started eating that, too.

With his mouth full, he spoke to Maggie, "Get more for my men!"

Maggie was relieved to be able to run out of the room on his command. There was more food but not much. Luckily, they had cooked four chickens earlier for the children's dinner. She shuttered to think of what those hoodlums would do if there was nothing to bring out.

She put the chickens on a plate and brought them to the dining room. One of the men grabbed the plate from her and brought it over to Gorticcio. He motioned for them to help themselves, and they began to pull the chickens apart and feast on them. Maggie noticed that they were all focused on the food, so she was able to slowly inch over toward the nuns in the corner of the room.

Just as she reached Sister Agatha, a series of arrows darted through an open window, across the room, and into the backs of four of the gang members.

As they fell to the floor, Gorticcio looked up, startled for a moment, and then watched while another series of arrows came through the same window and hit the chests of three other men. It all happened so fast.

Gorticcio pulled his gun and motioned to a few of his remaining men to go outside and to a few others to go to the window. He stood up and walked toward the front door, remarkably calm.

With the gang members otherwise occupied, Clark, the oldest boy, led the group of boys and girls quickly to the children's bedroom. Russell, the next oldest boy, lowered his head and dashed across the dining room to the corner and helped Maggie untie the nuns. The nuns ran to the children's room to keep safe watch over them.

Once the children were safely in their room and guarded by the other nuns, Sister Agatha and Maggie peered out, looking for a way to help.

The Indian warriors were aware of the advantage of silence for the surprise attack; the loud blasts triggered from the gang's muskets and rifles gave away their exact positions at all times. Arrows and spears were quiet, deadly, and efficient tools of ambush.

The bandits shot at the incoming warriors, managing to wound several of the Tommahoes, but even with their guns, they were no match for the Indian fighters.

Adam led a group of warriors into the orphanage through a back door. They quietly went through the hallway, split into three groups, and stormed the main room through the three doorways. The expertly aimed arrows hit their marks through the open doors of the dining hall, and the Gorticcio gang was wiped out.

After watching all of his men fall, Pedro Gorticcio ran from the room and through the front door in an attempt to reach his horse and escape, but Adam tackled him to the ground and began punching him.

Gorticcio fought back. He was on top of Adam, choking him, when a stream of arrows from all directions made their way into Pedro Gorticcio's body.

When the final arrow was released, Pedro Gorticcio lay lifeless on the ground. His gang lay dead inside. The reign of terror of Pedro Gorticcio and his men was finally over.

The children ran through the rooms opening all the windows and waving to the Indian warriors outside surrounding the orphanage.

Maggie burst out of the front door and through the crowd of Tommahoe warriors to her love and began to cry uncontrollably as she fell to the ground. She threw her arms around Adam and kissed every inch of his face.

The following day, everyone resumed the wedding preparations at the orphanage. Adam, Maggie, and Sister Agatha returned to Mount Dove to thank Chief North Star and his warriors for all their help.

CHAPTER 8

THE WEDDING

News of the demise of the Pedro Gorticcio gang traveled fast, and the town was indebted to their hero, Adam Starks, and his friend and ally, Chief North Star. With those thugs out of the way, Goldstone and the surrounding towns felt a tremendous sense of relief.

As the wedding day was approaching and final preparations were being made, many of the people in town felt obliged to contribute to the celebration and joy. Everyone turned out to help, and the contributions came pouring in.

The shattered wooden dining table in the orphanage had been replaced by a beautiful, solid oak table, hand-carved by Mr. Loomis and several volunteers. Tapestries and paintings were donated by artists from all over the county for the special occasion, in appreciation for their new feeling of security.

Talented musicians offered their services free of charge, and generous gifts were stacked up. Candles and flower arrangements were placed throughout the orphanage with elaborate displays in the dining room.

Many of the women in town offered to provide the food, and when the day finally arrived, the excitement was overwhelming.

Adam received a custom-made suit and shirt from the tailor and new shoes from one of the retail merchants.

Maggie's wedding gown was exceptionally elegant and fine. With the money she saved, she purchased European fabric and the finest pattern; her mother helped her sew it, with the most delicate finishing touches. Her shoes were imported, too, and with the simple flower headpiece she designed, Maggie felt like a princess the moment she got dressed.

The evening was finally here. Sister Agatha and the bride's and groom's parents greeted the guests as they streamed in. All were in their Sunday best.

The Professor was the first guest to arrive. He was immaculatedly dressed, clean shaven for the event, and in great spirits. He was followed by Mr. and Mrs. Davis, who were smiling from ear to ear.

Mr. Fitz made his way through the crowd; he was without his bodyguards, which was unusual for him. Harry and Peter, always in close proximity to their boss, were specifically not invited.

Mr. Fitz had invited his friend, Governor Tannin, who accepted the invitation, not wanting to miss a public relations opportunity.

While Fitz waited for Tannin to arrive, he mingled with Jack and James, the father of the groom. Ordinarily, Fitz never socialized with his workers, but Adam was the town's hero, and this was all good publicity for the mining business.

Mr. Fitz saw Adam across the room and was about to go over to congratulate him, when all of a sudden, there was a hush over the crowd. All eyes turned to the entryway to see a group of dignitaries and photographers enter the room. Then—they couldn't believe their eyes—entering the room was the most honored guest, the President of the United States of America.

The President was an imposing figure, nearly as wide as he was tall, with a full gray beard and moustache, rosy cheeks and a sparkle in his eye. He was elegantly attired in a dark blue three-piece suit, with a gold pocket watch dangling from his waistband.

The President was thrilled when he learned of the demise of the horrible Gorticcio and his gang, who were responsible for so much suffering across the country. He rearranged his schedule to be able to come to Goldstone to meet the heros. He also thought it was a terrific public relations move just before the upcoming elections.

A path cleared for him and his entourage; silence fell over the room as everyone stood staring at the incredible sight of their country's leader standing right before them.

Adam saw Maggie enter the dining room through one of the hallway doors. She was a vision of loveliness. He hurried over to her, grabbed her hand excitedly, and the two smiled as the President approached them, firmly shaking Adam's hand and delicately kissing Maggie's.

Then the President spoke as the crowd listened. "I am honored to be here with you tonight on such a special occasion. Adam, you have done an invaluable service to your fellow American citizens. You are a fine, upstanding young man who has helped bring justice to this town and to this country. I wish you and your lovely bride, Maggie, all the best as you enter into the blissful state of matrimony.

"I also want to extend this nation's gratitude to Chief North Star and the Tommahoe Indians for their bravery, sacrifices, and contributions to us all.

"And, of course, to Sister Agatha—you are one of a kind. May God be with you," and as he turned to the crowd, "and with all of you fine folks of Goldstone. God Bless America!

"And now, I plan to enjoy a bit of this fine food before the ceremony begins. Thank you all very much."

The crowd applauded, and the music began.

Maggie and Adam shook hands with the President again and thanked him for his kind words. Then they watched as he walked over to Sister Agatha to introduce himself.

Sister Agatha brought Chief North Star over to meet the President, and they shook hands as photographers pushed each other aside to get the best possible photograph.

Cameras flashed continuously, capturing the love between Maggie and Adam, the honor bestowed upon them by the President, and the joy of the guests to be included in this very special occasion.

A minister approached the podium set up on the stage and asked everyone to be seated. Maggie and Adam exchanged vows of love through eternity and kissed at the conclusion of the ceremony.

The crowd cheered and applauded as the musicians took up their instruments again and filled the room with wonderful music. Dancing began, and between do-si-dos and waltzes, everyone was in a state of sheer delight.

The President walked over to Maggie and asked for a dance with the lovely bride.

Just before the song began, Governor Tannin approached the President to extend his regards.

"So good to see you again, Mr. President. It's always such a pleasure to be in your company," the Governor said in a friendly tone.

"Yes, I'm sure it is," the President responded with a more formal attitude. "Thank you."

"Mr. President, I would be honored to introduce you to the business leader of this town, the man who made Goldstone what it is today, my good friend, Mr. Andrew Fitz."

Fitz forced his best smile and rushed over to the President to shake his hand. He extended his sweaty palm expectantly, but just then, a new song started, and the President turned toward Maggie.

"Oh, sorry, I must have this dance, you understand." He turned and escorted Maggie to the dance floor, as Mr. Fitz remained with his arm outstretched. Embarrassed, Fitz swiftly withdrew his hand and put it deep into his pocket.

Governor Tannin let out a deep sigh, mumbled something to himself under his breath, and walked away, while his right eye started to twitch nervously.

Fitz attempted to recover from his humiliation and called out, in the most confident voice he could muster, "Good to meet you, too, Mr. President."

But the President didn't hear him—he was immersed in the waltz and in his conversation with the lovely Maggie.

All eyes were on them as they danced, and despite his large size, the President was light on his feet and quite a lively dancer.

When the song ended, the President walked Maggie back to Adam, thanked her for the marvelous dance, and excused himself.

Adam escorted his bride to the front yard to breathe in the cool night air. It was a clear, beautiful night. The stars were out, and a cool breeze blew down from the mountains. They held each other close, looking deeply into each other's eyes. They felt as if cradled in the arms of the universe. They were one, and they were blessed.

Within a few days, word of their outstanding heroism spread across the nation. A photograph of Adam, Sister Agatha, and Chief North Star with the President of the United States would be the front page story in all the newspapers across the country.

CHAPTER 9

GOLDEN COMPLICATIONS

Maggie and Adam were very happy as they settled into their new life together. Although Mr. Fitz didn't give Adam all the bonus money that was promised for the gold discovery, he did get some; and Adam and Maggie were able to move into a small cabin just outside of town—their own home, at last.

Adam continued to work at the mines and was promoted to Assistant Foreman, which put him in charge of one of the crews each day, under Jack's supervision. James, Adam's father, was a foreman on another site at Goldstone Mines, and they were able to meet once in awhile for lunch when they were mining near each other.

Maggie continued to work at the General Store and was enjoying the pleasures of organizing their new household, planning their meals, making curtains, and decorating as best she could on their limited budget. They had received a lot of gifts at the wedding, and her parents and in-laws helped them out a bit, too.

The Professor came over once a week for dinner, and Maggie tested out all her new recipes then. Adam still helped out at the General Store on Saturdays, loading Sister Agatha's wagon and making deliveries to the orphanage, but most of his spare time was spent with the Professor.

Adam found that he had a talent for the analysis required in medical research, and he enjoyed his work there. He assisted the Professor in making adjustments to his magical medication, developing formulas appropriate for other types of illnesses. They combined the same basic substances but in varying amounts and tested it to see which formulas were effective on which diseases. Patients continued to line up for treatment, and the Professor was successful in saving the lives of many people who came from all over the country to see him.

As time passed, there was one thing missing in the otherwise happy marriage of Maggie and Adam—they yearned to have children.

During their courtship, they spoke often of wanting a large family. Adam was very close to his brothers and sister and enjoyed watching them grow up. Maggie was an only child and felt the loneliness of not having any siblings. Early on, Adam and Maggie had decided they would try to have as many children as they possibly could. But after three years of marriage, they were still waiting.

At every family occasion, their parents and friends would ask them, "When are you going to start a family? What are you waiting for?" Adam and Maggie always felt badly afterwards. They didn't want to discuss it with the family and didn't know what to say, so they quickly changed the subject.

One evening, when Adam was working with the Professor in the lab, he decided to seek advice. He explained how he and Maggie had been trying to have a baby since their wedding night, with no luck. They were very concerned and hoped the Professor could help them.

"Bring Maggie in for a check-up, Adam," the Professor said. "Let me see what I can do."

Later that week, Adam and Maggie came in to see the Professor, and he examined them. He found all of Maggie's test results to be normal. But when he put Adam's samples under the microscope, he noticed something very unusual. He tested the sample again, with the same results, and called Adam over to the microscope to see for himself.

The Professor explained to Adam what they were looking at. "Do you see these tiny fish-like 'swimmers,' Adam? They are your reproductive cells. Do you see how they all seem to be encased in a translucent, golden shell?"

Adam looked at the sample under the microscope and saw them for himself.

The Professor continued. "That golden outer shell should not be there. Let's dissect one cell and look more closely at it."

They isolated one of the cells, removed the shiny gold outer layer, and began to test the chemical composition. The Professor conducted his tests three times to confirm the results. Then he asked Adam and Maggie to sit down to discuss his findings.

"Well," he began, "I must say that I have never seen this particular condition in all my years of practice. I don't want to alarm you, but this is not only unusual but possibly irreparable. The shell Adam and I saw earlier appears to be a film of golden particles that have adhered to each reproductive cell. The gold film now forms a barrier around each cell.

"I believe the situation must be caused by the release of the gold in your bloodstream, Adam—a result of your injury at the mine.

"There may be a treatment option, but I hesitate to suggest it. I have no way of knowing if it will be successful or what complications may develop. And even if it did work, there may be complications during childbirth. It's very serious, indeed. I've cured many illnesses, but this is different, very different—a delicate situation."

The Professor paused for a moment, feeling very sad to have to say what he was thinking but knowing that he had to continued. "The more I consider the seriousness of the condition, the stronger I feel that the best solution is to do nothing. You're both young and healthy; you have a beautiful life together. Try to be content without having children. That's my recommendation."

Maggie and Adam were stunned. They looked at each other, as tears filled their eyes. Adam took Maggie's hand in his and spoke to the Professor.

"It's been our dream to have a family, Professor. Life just wouldn't be complete without children. You said there might be a treatment. If there's anything you can do, I think we're willing to try it, right, honey?"

He looked at Maggie; his beautiful wife was crying. He wanted her to have everything; it was just not possible to take away her dream of being a mother. Whatever it took, Adam was willing to do it.

Maggie looked back at Adam and responded, "Whatever we have to do, my darling." She knew how much Adam wanted to have a child—he'd be such a good father. She thought about how protective and caring he was with his brothers and little sister. They had to have a family of their own—they just had to!

The Professor saw their deep desire—these two wonderful people whom he loved as if they were his own children. Of course he would help them.

"If that's your decision," the Professor said, "I will do whatever I can. Let's get to the lab, Adam, and see if we can develop a vaccine which would dissolve the outer shell without harming the cell itself."

Adam responded, with excitement and hope in his heart, "Yes, I'm sure we can, Professor." Adam knew if the Professor put his mind to the task, he would find a solution to the problem, no matter how difficult or unusual it appeared.

"Thank you so much, Professor," Maggie added.

Maggie and Adam stood up and hugged each other. They were smiling, so relieved that the Professor was on the case.

The Professor worked on the formula for weeks, mixing bee pollen with citrus acid and various herbs and flowers, testing it on dozens of samples taken from Adam. The solution had to be strong enough to dissolve the golden casing, but gentle enough not to harm or change the cell inside in any way. It was a complicated and delicate situation.

After constant trial and error, they finally had what appeared to be the correct formulation. Adam watched, wide-eyed, as the Professor put an encased cell under the microscope and applied the medicine to it with an eye-dropper. They watched as the golden glass-like outer layer dissolved until it was gone, and the cell wiggled on its own.

Adam leaped into the air and let out a holler. "Yes, Professor, you've done it!"

The Professor smiled; he was happy to see Adam so excited. But then he thought about the possible complications. He put his arm around Adam and brought him over to the kitchen table, where they sat down.

"Adam, I just want to discuss the risks again with you. I know this looks very promising, but we can't be certain how the solution will react when it enters the human bloodstream. There could be a reaction to the medication; there could be effects from the golden particles when they dissolve." He asked again, "Are you sure you and Maggie want to take the risks?"

Without hesitation, Adam replied, "Professor, we've thoroughly discussed this, and we're sure. Maggie will be so thrilled to hear that we have it. I'll go now and tell her the good news. Thank you, Professor. We are so grateful to have you in our lives."

"Okay, Adam, I'll come by the house tomorrow evening, and we'll do the procedure. Don't eat or drink anything after midnight tonight."

"Fine, Professor. Thank you. We'll see you tomorrow." He rushed home to tell Maggie the news.

When he got home and explained everything to Maggie, they were so excited, they couldn't stop smiling all evening. The thought of finally having the chance to start a family was thrilling. They didn't eat or drink anything, and they didn't sleep a wink all night.

The next morning, Adam went to the mines as usual, coming home at around 4 p.m.; Maggie also worked as usual but left the General Store a little early, getting home at the same time.

The Professor was at their door an hour later with the medication in a syringe. He asked them to sit down for a moment so that he could review the procedures.

The Professor would be injecting them both with the potion. It would take about twenty minutes for it to hit their systems. "You'll both feel a warm sensation," he explained. "That's expected. And after that . . ." he smiled, "then . . . you may proceed."

He injected them with the solutions. Maggie and Adam both felt the liquid flow through their veins—warm, just like the Professor had said.

As soon as the procedure was complete, the Professor left.

The sunset over the mountains was extraordinary. Maggie and Adam stood by the bedroom window and watched with their arms around each other, wishing with all their might that their dream would come true tonight. Then they kissed and cuddled for the rest of the evening.

Two months passed, and Maggie was feeling a bit tired. Adam took her to see the Professor for a check up. After taking a blood sample to the backroom lab and testing it, the Professor came back with a big smile.

"I have wonderful news for you both. You're going to have a baby!"

Adam and Maggie were ecstatic, jumping up and down with joy. They hugged the Professor and each other, beaming with happiness. They could hardly believe it.

"Now, Maggie, my dear, you must get your rest and eat properly during the pregnancy. I'll be watching you closely; you'll need to come in for a check-up each week."

Maggie hardly heard the Professor's words; she and Adam were locked in each other's gaze. Adam replied, "We'll both be watching her closely, Professor. I'll make sure she takes good care of herself. Don't worry about a thing."

The months went by quickly, and Maggie never felt better in her life. When the time finally arrived to give birth, Adam took her by horse and wagon to the Professor's. It took twenty-eight hours for Maggie to have the baby. She was in excruciating pain the whole time, and at one point, the Professor was very concerned about Maggie, not sure if she would make it through.

In the final hours, she was running out of strength, and the baby was having difficulty coming out. The Professor increased the pain medication, while Adam held Maggie's hand and encouraged her to stay strong.

At last, the baby came. It was a boy. He cried out as he entered this world.

Adam looked up and silently thanked the heavens for this beautiful, wonderful gift. The Professor cleaned the baby and put him in Maggie's arms. She looked at her son with motherly love and said, "We'll call him 'Angel'."

Adam said, "Yes, he's our Angel."

And they loved him so.

CHAPTER 10

ANGEL

Adam and Maggie enjoyed their new life as parents, and they were very proud of Angel. Adam was working at the mines, and Maggie took Angel to work with her each day to the General Store. Mr. and Mrs. Davis didn't mind. Since they had no children of their own, they were happy to play with Angel while Maggie was busy around the store.

Angel was a very good baby. He hardly ever cried, and when he did, Maggie knew she had to feed him or change his diaper.

For Angel's first birthday, Maggie and Adam invited all their family and friends to their home for a party.

The Professor came, along with the Sisters from the orphanage, and Mr. and Mrs. Davis. Jack and a few of the other men from the Goldstone Mines came with their wives and girlfriends; and all of Angel's grandparents, aunts and uncles were there to celebrate the grand occasion.

Maggie and her mother had prepared all the food and decorated the house with flowers from the garden. Adam's brother, Jason, played the fiddle, while people sang along to the music and danced.

Maggie and Adam were very proud as their parents fussed over Angel, the first grandchild in the family. Angel was just starting to take his first steps, and everyone was impressed that he could already be so steady on his little feet.

As he inched his way across the room, all eyes were on Angel. Then, all of a sudden, his face turned red, and he let out a painful cry. Maggie, who was by his side, picked him up to comfort him. It was just an instant, and the discomfort passed.

Maggie carried him to the bedroom and said, "That's okay, my sweetheart. Mama will change you and everything will be all better again." Everyone turned their attention back to the party, smiling, as Maggie closed the bedroom door behind them.

She lay Angel on the bed to change his diaper. The used diaper was thrown into a bucket by the side of the bed to be washed later. She went over to the water pitcher and dampened a cloth, wiped Angel clean, tossed the cloth in with the soiled diaper, and put a fresh diaper on him. "We're ready to go back to the party, my little one," she said, as she picked up her baby boy and held him close. Angel was delighted, and with big smiles on both their faces, they returned to the festivities in the other room.

The party lasted well into the night, and by the time the last guest had left, Maggie and Adam were exhausted. They decided to leave all the cleaning for the morning and went directly to bed.

The next day, Maggie got up bright and early. Adam and Angel were still asleep. She quickly put the house back in order, washing the dishes, and rearranging the few pieces of furniture. She went back to the bedroom to get the diaper bucket.

Adam was just getting up, and she leaned over the bed to kiss him. "Good morning, my love," she whispered so as not to wake the baby.

"Good morning, sweetheart," Adam responded in a low voice. He went over to the wash basin in the corner of the bedroom and splashed some water on his face.

Maggie took the diaper bucket into the kitchen and got out a wash cloth. She began scrubbing the diaper and noticed something strange. The stains on the diaper and cloth seemed to be metallic. She touched them and looked at them more closely. How could this be, she wondered? It was the first time she had seen such a stain on one of Angel's diapers.

Adam was just coming into the kitchen as she turned around. "Adam, I want to show you something." He walked toward her, looking at the cloth she was holding in her hand. "Look at Angel's diaper from last night."

Adam took it from her and looked at it closely. "Maggie, what is this? It looks strange."

"That's what I thought, too, Adam. What is it?"

They were both silent as so many thoughts ran through their heads.

After a moment, Maggie walked toward the bedroom to check on Angel, and Adam followed her. They both looked down at their baby, sleeping so peacefully.

Maggie didn't want to disturb him, but she needed to see the diaper he slept in. She lifted him carefully and put him on the bed. Adam went over to the water basin and got a wet cloth, grabbed a clean diaper from the pile on the table, and went back over to Maggie as she took the soiled diaper off. She cleaned him up, put on the new diaper, and put Angel back in his crib. He had slept through the entire process. She fixed his blanket, and Angel cuddled in. He was sleeping so soundly, they tip-toed out of the bedroom, closing the door behind them.

Maggie had the newly soiled diaper in her hand as they walked to the window in the kitchen. They stared at it, seeing a stain glistening in the sunlight.

"Why don't I take this over to the Professor after work today, Maggie, and see what he thinks."

Maggie nodded and gave Adam the diaper. He put it away to take later.

"I'll keep a close eye on him today at the store."

"I better get going now, honey, but I'll see you tonight."

They kissed and Adam left for the mines. Maggie woke up Angel, fed him, did a few more things around the house, and took Angel to work.

Mr. and Mrs. Davis played with Angel as usual, and Maggie watched him all day. He seemed perfectly healthy and in very good spirits, but Maggie couldn't help worrying about him.

Adam was going through the motions at work, but his mind was focused on Angel, his beautiful son. He couldn't wait to see the Professor to get his opinion on the situation.

Finally, the shift ended, and Adam hurried back home to pick up Angel's diaper. Then, he went to see Professor Morgansteen. The Professor met him at the door and took the diaper to the microscope.

After examining it for some time, he came to a conclusion: "It's pure gold—no doubt about it; most unusual."

Adam couldn't believe what the Professor had just said. Gold, pure gold, coming from his baby boy!

"How could it be?" Adam asked.

"I don't know, Adam, but I have an idea. I need to see Angel right away. Bring him over now. I'd like to do some tests."

"Yes, Professor, I'll go get him."

Adam rushed to the General Store and told Maggie about his conversation with the Professor. She was shocked as well and didn't speak. Worrying all day about the possibilities of what seemed to be happening—it was all too much for her.

Adam held her close and comforted her. "Don't worry, honey. We've been through so much together; we'll get through this, too. I'll take Angel with me now, Maggie, and when you're finished here, come join me. It will probably take some time."

Angel had spent a lot of time with the Professor at various times in his first year of life—all the family get-togethers and the weekly dinners at the Starks' home. The Professor loved Angel like a grandchild, so when he saw Angel later that evening, it was more emotional than just a physician examining a patient.

He asked Maggie and Adam to leave Angel in his care, go home, and get some rest.

"We wouldn't be able to sleep anyway, Professor. We'd prefer to stay here," Maggie said.

"That's fine. I could probably use your help with the tests, Adam, and Angel might want his mother."

Then, with tenderness, the Professor took Angel to the examination table. All the while, the Professor was talking and singing to the child, tickling and laughing with the boy—making sure that Angel was distracted while the Professor took his temperature, and pulse, and drew blood. The evening went by quickly for all of them.

By midnight, Angel had fallen asleep. Adam and Maggie looked in on him as he slept peacefully. He was a beautiful boy. What was happening to him, they wondered?

Meanwhile, the Professor was in the lab testing the samples. He came out an hour later and said, "This is going to take more time. Let's all try to get some rest, and we'll resume in the morning."

"We'll be fine on the porch, Professor. Maggie and I will take turns watching Angel, while you get some sleep."

In the morning, Adam and Maggie had to go to work. The Professor asked that they leave Angel for another day or two, which would give him a chance to observe the boy's digestive system. Adam knew he couldn't take time off from the mines, but Maggie said she'd go to the store and ask Mr. and Mrs. Davis for some time off and come back as soon as she could.

During the day, the Professor continued the tests. Maggie had returned midmorning and kept herself busy by preparing lunch for the Professor. Angel was only allowed to have some clear soup and water.

All of Angel's vital signs were normal, but the Professor could see that Angel was straining to push the golden excrement out of his body. The baby's face would turn red, and he was obviously experiencing pain.

As soon as his shift was over, Adam rushed back to the Professor's house. By then, the Professor was able to explain more about Angel's condition to the anxious couple.

"The golden excrement hardens outside of Angel's body, and we must keep it that way. As time goes by, the gold may harden internally, and that could be fatal. I need to develop a vaccine to keep the substance fluid and easy to pass through his system. That's the first thing I must do. It may take a few days, but I promise I won't stop until I have it. In the meantime, you can take him home, but keep him on a liquid diet."

"Professor," Adam said, "what's causing this? Where is the gold coming from?"

"Well, I believe there is a molecular cause," the Professor explained. "It's basically in his genes. His body produces the chemical components of gold, and the gold gets eliminated from his body in the same way that the digestive system eliminates the waste, or by-products, of eating.

"I don't think this is a temporary situation. This seems to be his body make-up, which means that we need to develop a way for him to live with the condition. As long as his body can eliminate the gold as waste, while avoiding damage to his internal organs, he'll be okay. Let me know if you see any changes in the boy. I'll get started on that vaccine."

Adam and Maggie took Angel home and put him to sleep. They couldn't stop running the Professor's words through their minds. It was a permanent condition; they needed to avoid damaging internal organs; the gold could harden inside. They couldn't shut their eyes that night—afraid if they closed them, they might never see their baby again.

Adam and the Professor worked each evening trying to develop a medication for Angel. After an intense week of trial and error, they finally succeeded. The formula they created was digestible and would keep the gold fluid in Angel's system. It was still risky. After all, they had no one else to test it on before giving it to the baby. But there were no other options.

Maggie and Adam brought Angel to the Professor's when the formula was ready. The Professor had flavored the drug to make sure Angel would drink the golden colored liquid without too much fuss.

"Just make sure he drinks this with each meal," the Professor instructed. "We can't stop his body from producing the gold. But our main concern right now is to keep his body producing the gold as a fluid and getting rid of the waste in a natural manner, and this medicine will help him do that. We want to be sure it doesn't harden until it leaves his body. This medicine will keep the gold from hardening internally. For now, this is the best we can do.

"I will continue to research the possibilities for molecular reconstruction that would block the production of gold in his body, but I don't want to give you false hope. There's also the possibility that Angel might develop a resistance to the medication, so we have to watch out for that, too.

"If you notice that the boy is more tired than usual, or if the gold starts to harden outside his body more quickly, that's a sign that he's becoming resistant, and the medicine may no longer be effective. I'll begin to work on a stronger strength of this drug which we'll use in that event."

"I'll work with you, Professor," Adam replied. "See you tomorrow. Thank you."

They took their baby home, with a large supply of the life-saving liquid in hand.

CHAPTER 11

THE SCANDAL

As the weeks went by, Maggie and Adam adapted to their new routine, giving Angel his medicine with each meal and seeing the Professor regularly to get a supply of the drug as they needed it.

The medicine kept Angel from further harm. He had no pain and was a happy, active little boy. Maggie would wash his diapers in a bucket as usual and watch the gold sink to the bottom of the bucket. She collected the gold, which accumulated by the pound very quickly.

They decided to bury the gold in the backyard behind their house. They would put it aside each day, and once a week, Adam would wait for darkness and then go out to dig a hole to hide it.

They knew the gold was very valuable and over time could make them very rich, indeed. As the gold accumulated, Adam and Maggie couldn't help but wonder what life would be like to have this wealth. They dreamed of quitting work, traveling the world, taking care of all the people they loved.

But they didn't allow their thoughts to wander too long. They knew they would never be able to explain their new riches. If anyone were to know it's source, Angel's life could be in danger. Nothing was worth that risk.

So Maggie and Adam vowed not to touch their treasure. The only other person who knew of Angel's condition was the Professor, and he could be trusted to keep their secret. They also did not want to burden their parents or anyone else with the secret. They agreed no one else should ever know.

The secret became a part of their routine, and they were true to their promise: Adam buried the sacks of gold in the backyard, and they never touched them. Angel grew to be a healthy little boy, and with the help of the medication, no one suspected anything unusual.

Adam continued to get up early each morning, going to work at the Goldstone Mines, and Maggie continued at the General Store, bringing Angel with her each morning. She always made sure she was the one who changed Angel's diaper, although Mrs. Davis always offered to do it.

One day, as Mrs. Davis started to unbutton Angel's pants, Maggie jumped up, in a panic, and yelled, "No, Mrs. Davis. I'll do it. You don't have to."

"It's okay, Maggie," Mrs. Davis said, "I'd like to help."

Maggie found it hard to insist, but she had no choice. "Please Mrs. Davis. I'd rather you didn't."

She knew she had hurt Mrs. Davis' feelings and wondered how long they could continue to hide Angel's condition.

What would happen when he didn't use a diaper anymore? Angel was almost three years old already. Soon he would be off to school, and what would they do then? These were constant concerns.

Their best days were Sundays, when Maggie and Adam enjoyed their day off and would get together with their families. But they always made sure no one was around to see them when it came time to give Angel his medicine.

One Sunday night, after returning from dinner at Maggie's parent's, under the light of a bright full moon, Adam noticed through the kitchen window that the ground where he had buried a sack of gold the night before had been disturbed. He rushed over to the spot and saw that the bag was gone.

He immediately ran back to the house and called out to Maggie. "We need to leave here right now. Someone's found Angel's gold. Just pack up a few things, and I'll get the wagon ready."

They had discussed the possibility of having to leave Goldstone one day if their secret ever got out, but they didn't realize that day would come so soon. All the necessary arrangements hadn't been made yet, but there was no time for that now.

Adam dug up all the sacks of gold and hid them in the wagon. Several months earlier, he had built a concealed compartment underneath the wagon between the two large back wheels to hide the gold in case they had to leave.

Maggie made sure they had their full supply of Angel's medicine, some warm clothes, and some food. And when the wagon was loaded, they headed east.

They would look for a small town away from Goldstone, where no one knew them, and they could start a new life. They rode for several hours and then stopped to rest for the night.

Back in Goldstone the next morning, Miss Olson, the town gossip, was spending the day shopping in town. She stopped at the bank and traded some gold nuggets for cash. She bragged to the bank clerk about how lucky she was to have found gold while gardening in her backyard. "I might have hit a big one," she exclaimed to the clerk, with a wide grin.

"How exciting for you, Miss Olson, and very rare," said the teller. "You're very fortunate, indeed."

Miss Olson thanked him for the speedy transaction and was off to her shopping.

Everyone at the bank was talking all morning about Miss Olson's newly found riches. The bank manager told his wife about it when she stopped by to say hello.

The bank manager's wife mentioned it to her son when she went to bring him lunch at the Goldstone Mines.

He thought it was an amazing story to tell his supervisor, Jack, when he caught up with him after the lunch break.

Jack was just finishing a conversation with Mr. Fitz, and Mr. Fitz overheard the story.

Fitz asked Jack to bring the miner to his office and repeat the full story, just as the man's mother had told it to him.

Mr. Fitz didn't believe what he was hearing, and if it was true, he felt that the gold belonged to him. After all, the gold in Goldstone was in his domain.

He sent his bodyguard, Peter, to fetch Miss Olson, who was trying on hats at the retail shop in town.

"Why in the world would Mr. Fitz want to see me?" she asked, while her mind raced through different scenarios—could he be interested in her romantically, she wondered? She imagined herself as the wife of the richest man in town, running the mines side by side, dancing at company parties, entertaining important people at their beautiful home, touring Europe, and dining together in romantic restaurants. Now that she thought about it, he had been looking at her in church last Sunday.

As a woman who had yet to meet her mate, Miss Olson thought it was quite possible her time had come.

"Just come with me, Ma'am. He wants to see you immediately." And off they went.

Miss Olson entered Mr. Fitz's office, expecting a warm and wonderful welcome. Instead, she was greeted by an angry, red-faced man, ready to explode, who yelled in her astonished face, "NOBODY STEALS FROM ME!"

She nearly fell to the floor but managed to maintain her balance, and said, "What are you talking about, Sir?"

"I own the gold in this town, Madame."

At which point she interrupted him to say, "That's Miss . . . Miss Olsen."

"I know who you are, and if you think you can get away with this, Miss Olsen . . ."

"Get away with what, Mr. Fitz?" she asked, after gathering her composure.

"Where did you get that gold?" he asked.

"From my garden," she replied.

"Are they growing gold in Goldstone now, Miss Olson? That's a new one. I can just close down the mines and go into the farming business."

"Well, Sir, I found it, and that's all there is to it."

Fitz wouldn't let up. He kept repeating his questions, beating her down.

Miss Olson finally broke down in tears and told him the truth. She had seen her neighbor, Adam Starks, bury the sack on his property the night before and, being a naturally curious person, she went over to have a look. Before she knew it, she had dug up the gold and run home with it.

That made much more sense to Fitz. But how did Adam steal the gold from him? Fitz wondered about security procedures at the mines. He pressured Miss Olson for more information.

"What else can you tell me about Adam?" he asked.

"Well, he and Maggie spend a lot of time with that Professor Morgansteen. That much I do know. He's over there several evenings a week," she said.

Fitz remembered that the young man worked with the Professor part-time. He called out to his bodyguard, Peter, "Bring Adam Starks in here NOW!"

When Peter brought Jack into the office instead, Mr. Fitz asked, "Where's Starks?"

"Adam didn't come into work today, boss. I don't know where he is. I asked his dad, James, this morning, but he doesn't know either. We were going to finish the shift and head over to his house to look for him ourselves later."

"Well, you get back to work. I'll see if I can't find him myself." Fitz's anger had spread throughout his body.

As Jack walked back to the dig site, Fitz called out to Peter, "Get Harry, and saddle up my horse. We're heading out."

Harry Catcher and Peter Rays, his longtime bodyguards, could be called upon to get any job done and often were. In no time at all, the three men were on their way to Adam's house.

When Mr. Fitz and his men got to Adam's place, they broke down the door and saw that the house was empty. It was clear that Adam and his family had left in a hurry—the place was messy, with clothing strewn about.

"I think the woman works at the General Store," Harry mentioned, and off they went.

Meanwhile, Mr. and Mrs. Davis had been worried all morning and were obviously upset. Maggie had never missed a day of work without notifying them. They didn't know what to do.

Earlier in the day, Mr. Davis, who was in very poor health, stayed behind to mind the store, while Mrs. Davis had taken a ride out to Maggie's house.

When she didn't answer the door, Mrs. Davis went to Maggie's parent's place, but the only thing she accomplished there was to get them worried, too. They hadn't heard from the children and didn't expect to—just assuming they were both at work.

The Davis' were pacing around the store when Mr. Fitz and his men walked in.

"We're looking for Maggie and Adam," Fitz said.

"They're not here," Mr. Davis answered.

"We haven't seen or heard from them," Mrs. Davis said. "We're so worried about them," she added.

"Me and my boys will find 'em," Fitz replied, pretending to be concerned about their welfare but actually determined to see them hang.

They left the store, and once outside, Fitz turned to his men and said, “I need to see the Sheriff first. Wait for me here, and keep an eye out.”

The Sheriff’s office and jail was just down the street. Mr. Fitz walked in like he owned the place. Sheriff Dowling stood up immediately, extending his hand and greeting his friend.

“Well, hello, Andrew. Now, what brings you to town in the middle of the day?”

Ted Dowling owed his job to Andrew Fitz, who did everything in his power to get his old friend the position. This wasn’t the first time Fitz came looking for a favor in return.

“Ted, I have a problem with one of my workers, Adam Starks. I have reason to believe he’s been stealing from me.”

The Sheriff replied, “Adam Starks. That’s the kid who called the Indians to deal with Gorticcio a few years back instead of coming to me. I’ll never forgive him for that. But I never thought of him as a thief.”

“Yeah, well, it’s always the ones you least expect. Anyway, he’s run away, and we need to find him, Ted. I’d like you to get a posse together to help with the hunt.

“Also, that doctor, Professor Morgansteen—I think he may be in on it or at least may know where Starks ran off to, so bring him in for questioning. Keep him here until I get back. Okay, my friend?”

Sheriff Dowling couldn't refuse. "Whatever you say, Andrew. I'll go get him myself, and I'll wait for you here."

"Oh, and Ted," Fitz continued, "I'm offering a thousand dollar reward for the capture of Adam Starks. Get the word out."

"Good. That'll help me get some good trackers, Andrew. I'll go get the Professor and then work on the posse."

Both men left the building together. The Sheriff headed to the Professor's place, and Fitz returned to his men in front of the General Store.

"Let's go," Fitz called out to Harry and Peter. "The Sheriff's on the case. I want to get back to the office and talk with the kid's father, James."

Adam's father was stunned as he was questioned by Mr. Fitz about Adam's whereabouts.

"I know my boy, Mr. Fitz, and he would never do such a thing. Whatever's going on here, I'm sure it's just a misunderstanding."

"For your sake, I hope you're right," replied Fitz.

At sunrise, Maggie and Adam started to pack up their campsite and prepared to continue their journey to a new life. Maggie made some oatmeal for breakfast and went to get Angel's medicine from the wagon.

"Oh, no," Maggie cried out, "the jar cracked, and all the medicine's spilled out!"

Adam came running with Angel close behind. He looked at the jar in Maggie's hand, which had just a small amount left at the bottom.

"What are we going to do?" Maggie asked.

Adam realized they'd have to go back. "Maggie, we can't run. Even if the jar hadn't broken, it would only last us a couple of weeks. What would we do then? We have to go back, get the Professor, and ask him to come with us."

They both thought for a moment. "You're right, Adam. What were we thinking? He's the only one who can make the medicine for us."

They gave the small amount of remaining golden liquid to Angel with his oatmeal. Then they finished packing up the wagon and left.

They decided to go back to town through the northern mountains, where they felt it would be safer. The plan was to hide out in the mountains near the Professor's house and wait until nightfall, when Adam would be able to sneak in to see the Professor and ask him to join them.

While Adam, Maggie, and Angel were heading north, the Sheriff was heading directly to the Professor's place. He found the Professor with a patient and decided to wait. A few minutes later, the patient left, and the Sheriff spoke with the Professor privately.

"Professor, I have reason to believe that you are involved with Adam Starks and the theft of some gold from Goldstone Mines."

"I've done no such thing, Sheriff, and neither has Adam Starks."

"Well, that may be, but I'm asking you to come with me to answer some questions, and I'm not really asking, Professor. I'm telling you.

"Now, I don't know if you had anything to do with this or not, but Andrew Fitz thinks you do. And if you're innocent, then, all the more reason we need to talk to Adam. Where is he?"

"Well, I'm sure he's working at the mines as we speak," the Professor replied. "I don't expect to see him here until after his shift—about 4 this afternoon."

"No," the Sheriff responded, "Adam didn't show up for work today, and he's not home either. No one's seen him.

"Look, Professor, Mr. Fitz thinks you know something, and since he's had some gold stolen from the mines, he has a right to talk to you. I need to provide him that right, so just come with me."

When they arrived at the jailhouse, the Sheriff placed the Professor in a cell, and said, "I need to tend to a few things, but I'll be right back, and then we'll have a chat. I'll leave Deputy Johnson here to keep you company."

The Professor didn't like that at all, but he had no choice. He thought that once he and the Sheriff had a chance to talk, he could convince him that Adam was innocent and so was he; that they had nothing to do with the stolen gold.

The Professor assumed it had something to do with Angel's gold and knew he had to keep that to himself. He imagined Adam and Maggie on the run, with Angel—did they have enough medicine with them? How far did they get? Maybe they needed him, and now he was stuck behind bars. If only he could get out and catch up with them.

The Sheriff was addressing a crowd of men at the saloon. "We have reason to believe that Adam Starks has stolen some gold from Andrew Fitz and the Goldstone Mines. He's left town, and judging from their tracks, they're headed east. I know that some of you are expert trackers, and this is your opportunity to earn a thousand dollar reward for his capture."

That was a large sum of money, and they were all impressed. Each man in the group looked around, sizing up the competition.

"He's traveling in a wagon with his wife and small child and should not have gotten very far," the Sheriff added.

At the corner of the bar sat two men—brothers—who were professional bounty hunters and excellent trackers. John and Bob Hunt happened to be passing through Goldstone, visiting Bob's girlfriend, Louisa, who ran the saloon in town. They were between jobs right now and couldn't pass up the opportunity to make a quick buck. Tracking was their specialty, and it would be easy for them to track a slow moving wagon.

The brothers had heard enough, and while the other men stood around talking about how they'd team up, John and Bob Hunt put on their hats and headed out.

Maggie, Adam, and Angel arrived at the north mountain ridge. It was late afternoon as they set up camp. They found a level area surrounded by brush and shrubs on a path that could not be seen from the road. From that spot, they had a clear view of the town spread out below.

Without his medicine, Angel was not able to eat and was getting weaker. Maggie was able to give him some water, but that was all he could have. They could see he wasn't feeling well.

There were still a few hours to go before sundown, when Adam felt it would be safe to make his way to the Professor's.

Bob and John had started heading east, traveling fast on horseback. They arrived at an abandoned campsite—the place where Adam and Maggie had spent the night. Bob dismounted his horse and bent down to examine the marks more closely and determined that they headed north.

The men continued to follow the tracks north until the road forked—one path led west; one, north. It was still daylight, and they could easily see from the fresh tracks that the wagon they were following headed west, back to the town of Goldstone.

The Hunt brothers covered a lot of ground quickly, confident that they would soon catch their prey. They had done this so many times before.

As they rode, John called out to Bob, "This is the fastest thousand dollars we've ever made!"

"Yeah," Bob yelled back, as they both smiled with satisfaction and continued to ride fast.

It wasn't long before the Hunt brothers came upon a narrow trail turning off the road. They slowed down and saw the wagon wheel marks on the path. Following slowly and quietly, they came upon a small hidden area off the road where Adam and Maggie had set up camp.

When they got closer, they could see the wagon they had been tracking; it was just beyond the brush. They watched from a distance and saw Adam, Maggie, and Angel sitting on a blanket near the wagon.

Bob and John pulled their guns out and charged toward the campsite.

Adam and Maggie heard the horses and jumped to their feet. Maggie pulled Angel close to her as Adam ran toward the wagon to get his rifle. Bob and John were in front of them in no time, and when Bob fired several shots from his gun in the air, Adam ran back to stand in front of Maggie and Angel to protect them.

Bob and John quickly dismounted their horses and approached them.

"You're a wanted man, Adam," said Bob. "There's a thousand dollar reward for your capture."

"Our son is sick," said Maggie. "And we need to get him to a doctor. We will gladly give you more than a thousand dollars, if you just leave us alone and be on your way."

"So, it's true, then," said John. "You did steal that gold from Fitz. Exactly how much did you get away with?"

"I didn't steal any gold from Mr. Fitz," Adam replied.

"Yeah, well, tell it to someone who's listening," Bob said with a chuckle.

"Tie 'em up," Bob instructed, and John went to get the rope from his saddle.

"Wait just a minute," Maggie said, and she bent down to reach into her bag. She pulled out a diaper, which looked like a piece of white cloth. "Here," she said, "there's more than a thousand dollars worth of gold here. Just please leave us alone and be on your way."

Bob took the cloth from her and looked inside. The gleam of the gold put a smile on his face.

The brothers walked a few steps away together and huddled in conversation.

"What should we do?" asked John.

They thought for awhile, and Bob said, "I think we can get more reward money from Fitz. It looks like they stole plenty of gold from him. But, I don't want to stroll into town with all of them. Let's keep them here while we negotiate with Fitz. We have some gold to show him as proof."

"Okay," John said, "but the boy does look sick, and they could blame us if something happens to him; I don't think we should leave him here. What should we do?"

"We'll take him with us," Bob replied. "We can leave him with Louisa, and she'll get him a doctor in town."

They forced Adam and Maggie to sit down and tied them to opposite sides of a large tree trunk. Ignoring their pleas to be released, John told them they would take Angel to town to get him medical care and come back for them later.

Maggie and Adam were distraught and looked at each other with despair and hopelessness.

Just before they tied a bandana across her mouth, Maggie said, "Please look for Professor Morgansteen. He's the only one who can treat our son and save him."

"We'll do that, Ma'am," John said. "Don't you worry."

They took Angel with them and rode to town.

CHAPTER 12

FIRE

While the town of Goldstone was turned upside down with the Adam Starks scandal, it was an ordinary day at the orphanage, where they had heard nothing about it.

The children at the orphanage had gone off to school, and the Sisters finished their work in the fields early. Sister Agatha and Sister Mary cleaned up and got themselves ready to go to town. They had a long trip ahead of them.

They had heard of some land that was for sale farther up north—a farm of substantial size. Sister Agatha knew that if the orphanage was to survive, they needed to be self-sufficient. This land was supposed to be excellent farming property. It was a bit out of the way, tucked in between the mountain ranges, but if they could develop an abundant crop there, it would be worth it.

Of course, they didn't have the money to buy anything at the moment. The summer weather had been extreme that year—a drought followed by floods—and it was the same situation the year before. The crops had severely suffered, and they had very little to sell.

So many people were struggling, donations were meager, too. Most of the townspeople could hardly feed and cloth themselves and their families these days and couldn't afford to give.

The Sisters knew they would need some financial assistance in order to keep the orphanage going. And there was only one person they could think of who was in a position to be so generous—Andrew Fitz. After all, he was the richest man in town. And he seemed to be very nice when they met him at Adam and Maggie's wedding a few years earlier.

Since then, he had made small donations from time to time, which seemed more for the sake of appearances than anything else. But this would require a significant donation, and once word got out, his generosity would be well known throughout the community. With that in mind, Sister Agatha felt that he could surely be swayed. And that's how she decided to approach the matter with him.

They felt it would be best if Sister Mary and Sister Agatha went to meet with Mr. Fitz in person to ask for his help. And they just wouldn't take no for an answer.

First, they needed to meet with the property owners. Sister Mary had heard that the elderly woman who lived there had passed away, and now her children, who had moved to San Francisco awhile back, wanted to sell it fast.

Since the wagon and horses were in use at the orphanage, Sister Mary and Sister Agatha took two mules and headed north to meet with the owners of the farm. After that, they would pay a visit to Mr. Fitz.

When the Sisters arrived at the farmland, everything they had heard about it was true—it was magnificent, and the soil was rich. The mountains shielded the crops from the summer's blazing sun, and the valley below absorbed the overrun of rain. It was a perfect spot for farming.

They stood there in the afternoon sunlight, enjoying the crisp early autumn breezes in the air. Suddenly, they heard several shots ring out. The Sisters could tell that it was coming from close by, just over the next ridge.

Sister Agatha turned to Sister Mary and said, "You stay here with the mules. I'll run over and see what's going on."

Sister Agatha hurried up over the mountain to the other side. When she got to the top, she saw a wagon and two horses below, off the road and behind some bush.

She went down the mountain, and as she got closer, she saw two men riding away. They did not see her. She continued down the mountain toward the wagon and then spotted Adam tied to the tree.

He saw her, too, but couldn't yell with the gag on his mouth. Agatha ran toward him and then saw that

Maggie was tied to the other side. She quickly untied them.

"What happened?" Sister Agatha asked. "What are you doing here?"

"It's a long story, Sister," Adam replied. "But we don't have time now to tell you all the details. In short, I've been accused of stealing gold from Mr. Fitz, but it's not true.

"More importantly—these two bounty hunters, who were looking for me, have taken Angel. And Angel is very sick. The only one who can help him is the Professor. We need your help."

Maggie added, "We have to go after those men and get Angel back, and we need to get the Professor."

Sister Agatha had no doubt of Adam's innocence and was very concerned about Angel. She asked no questions, knowing they had to move fast. She told them that Sister Mary was with her. "She's just over the hill. I'll go with her to find the Professor."

"Good," Adam said, "Maggie and I will go after Angel."

Maggie and Adam unhooked the horses from the wagon and were quickly on the trail in pursuit of the Hunt brothers.

Sister Agatha met up with Sister Mary, and they traveled as fast as they could on the mules toward the Professor's house.

When they got to the Professor's, he wasn't there. They rushed over to Adam's parents, who had just found out that the Professor was in jail.

The Sisters told them the story just as Adam had told it to them—bounty hunters taking Angel, the reward money being offered for Adam's capture, and how they needed to get the Professor.

"They need Angel's medicine," Sister Mary added.

"Is Angel sick?" Adam's mother asked.

"Yes," Sister Agatha replied, "he's very sick, and they said the Professor would know what to do."

James asked, "What can I do to help?"

Sister Agatha thought for a moment and said, "We need fresh horses, and we have to hurry."

When the Sisters walked through the front door of the jailhouse, they found the deputy sitting in a chair, with his hat over his face, taking a nap. Behind him was the cell where the Professor was laying on a cot.

Sister Agatha pulled out the small hand gun she always carried under her robes, while motioning to Sister Mary to guard the front door.

She approached the deputy with the gun drawn. "Mr. Johnson!" she said loudly. The deputy was startled and almost fell off his chair, as he jumped up and pulled the hat off his face. "Please unlock the cell—and hurry. I'm not afraid to use this, so don't give me cause to."

The Professor jumped to his feet and grabbed his hat. The young deputy was surprised to see the Sister there with a gun and instinctively walked toward the cell, reaching down for the keys that were dangling from his belt. But then it occurred to him—she wouldn't shoot. He slowly turned toward her, with a smile on his face, and went to pull the gun from his holster.

Without a moment's hesitation, Sister Agatha shot the gun from his hand. "Unlock the door now, Deputy, and hurry. A child's life is at stake." He quickly opened the cell door.

They put the deputy in the cell, locked the door, and ran outside.

Behind the jail, in a narrow alley, Adam's father was waiting with horses. "I'll take care of the mules," he said. "Just get there safely."

The Sisters and the Professor arrived at the Professor's place. He quickly hooked up two horses to his wagon and loaded it with much of his lab equipment. With the Sisters riding beside him, they left in a hurry.

Not long after, the Sheriff made it back to the jail. Shaking his head in disgust, he unlocked the cell and let the deputy out.

Adam and Maggie followed the Hunt brothers' trail back toward town. It was getting dark now, but they were on track. Following a safe distance behind, they managed to catch up with them just outside of town. Maggie and

Adam took cover behind a row of stores while they watched the men enter the saloon. John was carrying Angel, and they could see that their son was very weak.

Bob and John walked into the saloon, and Louisa greeted them as they came through the door. "Hello, fellas," she said, as she and Bob embraced.

"Hi, Louisa," Bob said warmly. "We need a big favor."

"I have no money to give you," she answered. Every time he came to town, Bob asked her for a loan which he never repaid.

"This time, I might have money to give you," he replied. He turned around and took Angel from John's arms, handing him over to Louisa.

"What's this—a gift for me?" she asked. "How did you know I always wanted a little boy!"

"No time for jokes, honey, and don't ask any questions; just take care of him," Bob replied. "The kid is sick."

"Who is he?" she asked. "What are you guys up to?"

"I said no questions. Just take him upstairs. We'll be back later with a doctor," Bob said, as they left.

Louisa held Angel close as she took the boy upstairs. She spoke kindly to him. "Hi, little fella. What's your name?" Although his eyes were open, he was too weak to respond. "You'll rest awhile. I have a nice comfortable bed for you."

She took him to her room, put him gently on the bed, covered him with the blanket, and said, "You rest, and I'll be right back." Angel closed his eyes as Louisa closed the door behind her.

As soon as they saw the Hunt brothers leave the saloon without Angel, Maggie and Adam hurried in. As they entered, they saw Louisa coming down the stairs. Adam pulled the gun from his holster, and they approached her.

"Where's the boy?" Adam asked.

"No need for the gun, Mister," Louisa responded.

But Adam kept the gun drawn and pointed at her.

She hesitated and then said "The boy's upstairs, and I'm supposed to keep him here until the doctor comes."

Adam pushed her aside as he hurried up the stairs, with Maggie following. As they ran up, Louisa was behind them.

Maggie explained, "He's our son, and they took him from us. He's not well and needs his medicine."

"I knew those guys were up to no good," Louisa replied.

When they reached the second floor, Louisa brought them into the room where she'd left the boy. Maggie and Adam eagerly ran over to their son. But their joy was instantly replaced by worry—they saw how weak

Angel had become. They needed to see the Professor immediately and get that medicine.

Louisa could have called out for the saloon's guards—there were men who would have immediately overpowered the couple—but she knew the boy was seriously ill, and her heart went out to them. She told them to take their son but to tie her up first so it looked like she put up a struggle. She certainly didn't want Bob to think she had just let the boy walk out of there. But that's exactly what she did.

Adam held Angel in his arms as they ran down the stairs and outside to their horses.

After leaving Louisa, Bob and John Hunt went to see the Sheriff in town to notify him that they had captured Adam.

When they walked into the jailhouse, they saw a heavy-set man yelling at the Sheriff, "YOU CAN'T EVEN KEEP AN OLD MAN IN JAIL WHEN TWO NUNS WALK IN!" Fitz was screaming.

The Sheriff replied, "Andrew, they just left about fifteen minutes ago. We can catch up with them. They're probably on their way to the orphanage."

Fitz interrupted him, talking more to himself than anyone. "And that Sister Agatha, how dare she interfere in my business, after all those donations I've given her and that orphanage of hers."

"I know, I know," Sheriff Dowling agreed, "and I bet she's hiding Adam there, too."

"I don't think so, Sheriff," Bob interrupted, as he and John walked through the jailhouse door.

"Who are you?" asked Mr. Fitz.

"Bounty hunters, Sir," Bob replied, as he approached Mr. Fitz and extended his hand. Andrew's two bodyguards, who had been standing off to the side, stepped forward and stopped Bob in his tracks.

"It's okay, guys," Fitz said. "Let the man speak. So where is he?" Fitz asked. "Have you come for the reward? You should know that to get the payoff, you need to bring in the bounty," Fitz added.

"That's just it, Mister, we have him, but we don't think a thousand dollars is an adequate reward."

"What do you mean?" Fitz replied. "How dare you . . ." but he stopped when he saw Bob put his hand in his pocket. Fitz held his breath for a moment, on guard against this stranger. But when Bob pulled out a cloth from his pocket, Fitz relaxed.

Bob unwrapped the cloth and revealed the gold. "We got this from Adam, and it seems like they've stolen a lot more than a thousand dollars from you," Bob said. "You have to be fair, Mr. Fitz."

Fitz looked at the gold and reached over to grab it, but Bob quickly withdrew his hand and slipped it back into his pocket.

"What do you think is fair?" Fitz asked.

"Five thousand dollars." Bob replied.

"Five thousand?" Fitz yelled back. "You're a thief yourself!"

"Well," Bob continued, "that's the price if you want him back."

After a moment's pause, Fitz said, "Alright, you'll get your price. Where is he?"

"First," John interrupted, "we have his son at the saloon. He's not doing too well and needs a doctor—a Professor Morgansteen. And we have Adam and his wife tied up to a tree in a hideout outside of town. We can take you there."

"Don't you know?" the Sheriff said. "The Professor broke out of jail, and we're looking for him ourselves."

"But now," Fitz added, "since you have Adam, we don't need the Professor anymore. Let's go get him, and then you'll get your money."

Mr. Fitz and his two bodyguards, the Sheriff and four deputies, and the Hunt brothers were outside about to mount their horses, when a group of men from the posse, who had been out hunting for Adam, approached them.

"Adam's tracks are leading back to town, Mr. Fitz," one of the men called out.

"No," Bob said, "we left them tied up in the north ridge."

"We followed the tracks to that spot and saw the campsite," the tracker replied. "The rope around the tree was cut. The wagon's there, but the place is deserted. They came back to town, I'm telling you."

"They must have come back for the boy," Bob said. "He's in the saloon."

They all headed over there.

They found Louisa upstairs with her mouth gagged and hands tied behind her back. Once they released her, she told them that Adam and Maggie had left about twenty minutes earlier.

The Sheriff and Mr. Fitz stood in the saloon, frustrated. Fitz was really starting to boil now, having run all over town like an idiot, chasing these thieves.

"I suggest we split up," the Sheriff said. "Andrew, you and your men go directly to the orphanage and see if Adam went there. And I'll go with my deputies and the posse back to the campsite and see if there are any clues there."

John Hunt said, "My brother and I will go with you, Sheriff."

As Mr. Fitz and his men rode to the orphanage, all Fitz could think about was Sister Agatha and how she was making a fool of him. How could she do this to him . . . him of all people! She pretended to respect him, but now, she was helping a thief get away with his gold. This thought enraged him.

When they arrived at the orphanage, it was early evening, and the Sisters were in the dining room with the children. They banged on the door, and when one of the Sisters opened it, they pushed their way in.

"We're looking for Sister Agatha and Adam Starks," Fitz said.

Not waiting for a reply, Peter and Harry raced through the halls searching every room. After failing to find them anywhere, Mr. Fitz turned to the nuns and children, who were all huddled in the entryway, and screamed, "WHERE ARE THEY? If you give them up, nobody will get hurt."

When no one responded, Fitz gave the nod, setting his men into motion, and they ransacked the place.

They stormed through the orphanage in all different directions, flipping over the tables, breaking the dishes in the kitchen, ripping the children's drawings off the walls, throwing chairs through shattering windows, hooting and hollering as they went about.

After a few minutes of terror and destruction, Fitz raised his hand, signaling Harry and Peter to stop. The room fell silent as he asked again, "Where are they?"

He paused and stared at the frightened group of children and nuns with steely, sinister-looking eyes. He could no longer contain his anger. He screamed, "DON'T BE FOOLISH!"

One of the Sisters answered, "We don't know, Mr. Fitz. Sister Agatha was supposed to be back hours ago."

"I don't believe you!" Fitz snapped back at her. "You must know that she helped the Professor escape from jail, and she's probably around here somewhere, hiding with that thief, Adam Starks. And if he's not here, where did he go?"

The Sisters were shocked to hear this and did not respond. Fitz was furious and seething with rage.

"Fine," he said, and nodded again. With that, his men lit torches and hurled them at the walls. The window curtains ignited instantly.

"That will teach Sister Agatha not to interfere in my business!"

The three men left the building as the flames spread through the structure. In all of the chaos, the nuns were attempting to keep everyone calm as they led the panicked children out of the burning building to safety. Within minutes, the structure was totally engulfed in the blaze.

The flames were enormous and bright against the darkness of the evening, and the smoke forced the Sisters and children to stand back.

Just as the fire reached the far corners of the building, and Fitz was about to give the order to burn the lumber shed, a deputy arrived on horseback with a message from the Sheriff for Mr. Fitz.

"Sir," he said, "the Sheriff wants you to know that he's on Adam's trail. He wants me to take you to him."

Peter and Harry stared at the fire as Fitz motioned for them to leave.

The Sisters and children were left huddled outside, watching the orphanage collapse. The building went up so quickly, there was no way for anything to be saved. Everything perished.

Fitz and his men rode with the Deputy and met up with the Sheriff at the deserted campsite in the mountains.

"Andrew, we've found two sets of trails—one with the markings of a wagon, which we know belongs to Adam. They came back here from town to pick up their wagon—you can see the tracks are headed north. I think we should follow them.

"The other markings are over by the Professor's house. He's traveling in a wagon, and judging from the tracks, it's a pretty heavy load. We checked his place, and it looks like he took equipment with him from the lab. And there are two folks on horseback with him—probably the nuns. I've already sent the Deputy with a few men to follow the tracks. I'm confident that we can catch them, Andrew."

"Well, let's get on with it, then," Fitz replied, impatiently.

Meanwhile, as evening fell, the Sisters and Professor Morgansteen crossed the river of Valley Creek and climbed the foothills of Mount Dove. They were recognized by an Indian scout, who alerted the Chief that friendly visitors were coming. The Chief greeted them as they arrived at the campsite, and they told him all about the events of the day.

About a half hour later, the Indian scout spotted Deputy Johnson and four of his men approaching. Chief North Star sent ten of his warriors, under his son's command, to meet them as they crossed the river.

The Deputy addressed Wildwind, "I've come to arrest Professor Morgansteen, who's wanted for questioning by the Sheriff; and Sister Agatha and Sister Mary for helping the Professor break out of jail. I believe all three of them are hiding out at your campsite."

"It is true. They are here, and they are our guests," responded the Chief's son.

"You are interfering with the law," Deputy Johnson replied. "Now, let us do our job and release them to us."

"This is our land, Deputy, and there is only one law here. We do not honor your laws. Now, go."

"I have respect for your father, Wildwind, but you need to listen to me. If you don't release these people to us now, we will be back with a court order, and you'll be charged as an accomplice."

The Chief's son did not respond. It was clear that he would not budge. Deputy Johnson turned his horse around and rode back to town with his men.

After Maggie and Adam picked up their wagon from the north ridge, they road down mountains and through valleys, across rivers and flatlands—Adam, holding Angel close in his arms, and Maggie at the reins. They rode as fast as they could and were afraid that Fitz and his men were getting closer. To throw them off their tracks, they decided to make a detour and go farther north. They rode all night, and just before dawn, when they felt they were far enough away, they decided to rest for a short time.

Maggie wrapped Angel in Adam's coat and put him on a blanket to rest. He was very weak. She gave him some water from their canteen. They could tell that his condition was getting even worse. Without his medication, Angel was being poisoned by the gold inside of him, and his skin had turned a pale yellowish color.

At daybreak, Adam and Maggie were ready to continue to Mount Dove. They were several hours away and weren't sure if all the detouring helped. Maggie made a bed for Angel in the back of the covered wagon and stayed with him, while Adam sat up front steering the wagon.

They rode as fast as they could, and a few hours later, just before they crossed the river of Valley Creek, Maggie yelled to Adam, "I see horses coming from behind—about a hundred yards away."

Adam pushed the horses even harder, riding faster. As soon as they crossed the river, Mr. Fitz and his henchmen, with the Sheriff at their side, caught up and quickly surrounded the wagon, forcing them to stop.

Harry jumped into the wagon from the back, grabbed Angel, and pushed Maggie out. The Sheriff's men pulled their guns out and pointed them at Adam.

"PLEASE LEAVE MY SON ALONE," Maggie screamed.

"You stole the gold from me, Starks, and now you must face the consequences," Fitz said.

"Adam Starks, you're under arrest," said the Sheriff. "I'm taking you in."

But just then, Chief North Star and fifty Indian warriors emerged from the trees around them, with guns and bows and arrows drawn.

Fitz looked around and realized they couldn't fight them and win. He looked at the Sheriff and said, "Do something, Ted."

Chief North Star came forward and said, "Don't force us to fight you, Sheriff."

"Chief, we're here to arrest Adam for stealing, and we need to bring him in."

"You're wrong, Sheriff," the Chief responded, "and we won't let you take an innocent man to jail. Now, please give the boy back to his mother and leave peacefully."

Maggie rushed to grab Angel back from Harry and got back on the wagon with Adam. A few of the Indians came forward and surrounded the wagon to protect them.

The Sheriff knew the Chief was a man with strong convictions; there would be no negotiating with him. He turned to Fitz and said, "Sorry, Andrew, we're outnumbered, and we'll have to come back another time.

Fitz was out of his mind with anger; his face turned red. "I'll be back," Fitz said, "and I'll have you all arrested. Besides," he added, "the whole mountain is up for sale at auction next month, and I'm planning to buy it. Everything on it will belong to me, including your camp. So, we'll see who wins in the end, Chief." He turned around and said, "Let's get out of here."

And all the men followed, leaving the same way they came.

CHAPTER 13

REFUGE

The Indian warriors, led by Chief North Star, accompanied Adam and Maggie as they hurried up to the top of Mount Dove. When they arrived at the camp, the Professor was there waiting for them. He ran toward them and waved, pointing to the Chief's tent. Adam, with Angel in his arms, ran into the tent, where the Professor was ready with the medicine in hand; Maggie followed.

They placed Angel on the Chief's bedroll to rest. The Professor gently eased the medication into Angel's mouth with a dropper. The boy swallowed, coughing as the golden colored liquid went down his throat. Gradually, he was able to swallow a larger amount.

Within a short time, the yellowish tinge on Angel's skin began to fade, and his normal coloring returned.

"He will rest now for a few hours, and he should regain some of his strength by midday," said the Professor. They stayed with Angel for a few more minutes and watched as he fell into a restful sleep.

The Chief had been waiting outside. "How is the boy?" he asked.

"He'll be okay," the Professor responded.

"Thank you, Chief, for all you've done for us," Adam said.

"It's nothing, my friend. I'm glad you came to us. Now come with me. Let's wash up; food has been prepared."

"We have so much to tell you, Chief."

"There will be time for that, Adam," the Chief responded, as he motioned to the tribe's medicine woman. "She will stay by Angel's side while we eat."

Soon, they were sitting in the Chief's tent with Sister Agatha and Sister Mary, the Chief's son, Wildwind, and daughter, Nema, with her husband, Temo, and several other elders from the Indian tribe.

After the food was served, everyone was anxious to hear why Adam and Maggie were running from the law.

Adam began by saying that he was being accused of stealing gold from the mines, and since it would be hard to explain the gold that was found in their backyard, they decided to run.

"We've accumulated a substantial amount of gold," Adam said, "and this gold came from our son, Angel. I will let the Professor explain more about it."

Everyone in the tent was totally confused and looked to the Professor.

"About seven years ago, as you all know, Adam had an accident in the mines. In his fall, he was injured by a shard of gold rock which pierced his upper leg.

"I was able to cure his injury, but remnants of the gold traveled through his bloodstream and remained in his body. I believe this caused a condition in Adam's body that was transferred to his son, affecting the biochemical make-up of Angel's digestive system. Simply put, his system turns the food he eats into gold."

The Professor went on to explain the condition and the treatment in detail. "It's most unusual—probably one of a kind," he concluded.

Everyone was quiet for a moment while they tried to comprehend the magnitude of the situation. Adam looked around the tent at all the stunned faces and then said, "I know Maggie and I are among good friends here, and we feel safe with you. If the outside world were to know about this, the life of our son would be in danger.

"There are people out there who would be after Angel, looking to exploit him. The law in the town of Goldstone is controlled by the Governor and Mr. Fitz. They are not good people and can't be trusted to protect us; we can't put our lives in their hands. We need time to figure out how to get legal protection some other way so we can prove our story is true."

"We'll help you in any way we can," Chief North Star said. "Stay with us for as long as you need to."

"Thank you, Chief," Maggie replied. "We're so grateful."

At that moment, two Sisters from the orphanage came running into the tent. They had come to deliver the terrible news. "The orphanage was burned to the ground. No one was hurt, but there's nothing left."

Sister Mary burst out in tears. Sister Agatha was stunned, but she held herself together. She was extremely angry when she heard it was Mr. Fitz. Why would he do such a thing? And to think she wanted to turn to him for help to buy the land. She had certainly misjudged him. But at times like this, Sister Agatha knew she had to keep her composure.

She immediately turned to the Chief and asked him to help her organize a wagon-load of supplies. The Chief and his tribe prepared loads of food, clothing, tee pees, and blankets. By early afternoon, a small convoy of supplies were on their way to the children, who had been staying in the lumber shed.

Over the next several days, more food and supplies were delivered to the children by their Indian friends.

As the days passed, Adam, Maggie, and the Professor took turns watching Angel, who was gradually getting stronger with the medication. Angel's gold continued to accumulate and was being stored in a spot in the woods near the camp.

During the week, the routine at the Indian camp fell back into rhythm. Adam spent time with Temo hunting and fishing. Maggie helped Nema and the women with food preparations and their various chores. And as Angel felt stronger, he spent time with the children of the tribe, playing and learning. Adam and Maggie were just so happy to see Angel back to his old self.

The Professor had resumed his work, too, setting up a make-shift lab in one of the tents the Chief provided for him. He spent time with the old medicine woman and enjoyed her tales of ancient remedies and the spiritual conversations they shared.

The Professor helped many of the Indians overcome ailments they had suffered with for years. And as usual, a line formed at the entrance to his tent, as people waited for treatment.

Adam and Maggie's family came to Mount Dove to visit. They were so happy to see them safe and sound. Maggie and Adam took their parents aside and told them about their grandson. They were stunned by the revelation but relieved that the medication was working. Adam asked them not to mention anything to anyone.

"What are you going to do, son?" asked James. "You know the whole town is buzzing about you and the stolen gold."

"We always knew it couldn't be true," Adam's mother added.

"I'm not sure what we should do," Adam replied.

"If we can help you in anyway, we're here for you," Maggie's father said.

They spent the entire day together and made plans to return the following Saturday.

The next day, in the early afternoon, Sheriff Dowling arrived at the mountain. He was carrying a court order that called for Adam's arrest for stealing gold from Mr. Fitz, and for the arrest of Sister Agatha, Sister Mary, and the Professor for breaking out of jail.

He also delivered a warning to Chief North Star. "If these people do not turn themselves in within seventy-two hours, an arrest order will be issued for you, Chief, for interfering with the law."

Then, the Sheriff added, "Also in three days, Mount Dove will be put on the auction block; and when it's sold, you and the entire tribe will have to vacate or be considered trespassers."

After the Sheriff left, the Chief gathered everyone to discuss the situation. Chief North Star explained that he had heard three months ago that the State was going to put Mount Dove up for sale.

"Why not go to the auction, yourself, Chief?" Sister Agatha asked.

"We have no chance against a powerful man like Mr. Fitz," said the Chief. "I have been told that we have rights as current residents. If we pay five thousand dollars, we would have first claim on the land. We wouldn't even have to go to the auction, if we pay the money in advance; but we don't have it.

"The deer and buffalo have been so scarce this past year, and the crops so poor, we had just enough to feed ourselves. We had nothing to sell except the baskets, which didn't bring in much. It looks like our tribe will have to find another home . . . again."

"You have to let us help you," Maggie said.

"This is an emergency, Chief," Adam added.

Adam and Maggie suggested that Chief North Star use the gold they had collected from Angel to buy the mountain for his tribe.

"I can't do that," the Chief responded. "It would not be right."

Maggie pressed on. "Without your help, Chief, our son would probably not be alive today. You must take this gold, and use it to secure your tribe's future. It's the least we can do to repay your kindness and friendship."

Adam added, "You owe it to your people, Chief, and you must act fast. Get the money in before the auction."

The Chief was an honorable man and would not ordinarily take money that wasn't his, but Maggie and Adam made sense, and his responsibility to his people left him no choice. "We will repay you as soon as we can," the Chief concluded, with gratitude.

The next day, in the early morning hours, Chief North Star left Mount Dove and began his journey to Sacramento, with his son, Wildwind, and son-in-law, Temo, by his side.

Several hours later, they walked into the Town Clerk's office in Sacramento with five thousand dollars in gold. The Chief put the sack on the counter, as the Clerk looked at him suspiciously.

After processing the payment and completing the paperwork—and with some hesitation—the Clerk had no choice but to issue a Certificate of Ownership to Chief North Star and his Tommahoe Indian tribe.

With smiles on their faces and joy in their hearts, they rode back home to their mountain.

CHAPTER 14

SURROUNDED

When Mr. Fitz heard that the auction was canceled and the mountain had been sold to the Indians, he exploded. He stormed into the Governor's mansion to see his old friend, Governor Tannin, to demand justice.

Bristling with anger, he screamed, "THEY BOUGHT THE MOUNTAIN WITH THE GOLD THEY STOLE FROM ME! You have to fix this, Jeffrey. You owe me!"

Before long, Governor Tannin was on his way up to Mount Dove, with two of his aides, to address the situation.

Chief North Star welcomed the Governor up to the campsite and asked that his aides not be present during their conversation.

"We'd like to meet with you privately, Governor," the Chief said. "There are confidential issues to be discussed." The Governor had no objection.

The two men walked toward a tent, where Adam and Maggie, Sister Agatha, Sister Mary, and Professor Morgansteen were waiting.

"I've come here to sort out this situation, which has become very serious and urgent," the Governor said.

"As a matter of fact, it has come to my attention that the gold used to purchase Mount Dove was stolen property belonging to Andrew Fitz. This makes the sale of Mount Dove to the Tommahoe tribe null and void and transfers the ownership of the mountain to Mr. Fitz.

"I also must warn you, Chief," the Governor continued, "I have three thousand troops under my command, which I won't hesitate to call upon to take the mountain by force, if you and your tribe don't leave Mount Dove peacefully. "I have arranged to give you an additional seventy-two hours to evacuate. And let me remind the rest of you that you are listed on an arrest warrant and must turn yourselves into the Sheriff's office by the deadline, and that's tomorrow, by midnight."

The Chief didn't like the Governor's threats and took it as a sign of disrespect. He remembered his father telling him years ago that people who do not respect others should not be trusted, but he decided to reserve judgment.

"Hold on there, Governor Tannin," Maggie interjected. "Aren't you going to hear our side of the story?"

"Of course," replied the Governor. "That's what I'm here for."

Maggie and Adam looked at each other, and Adam said, "Please excuse us for a moment, Governor. My wife and I need a few minutes alone." The Governor nodded.

The couple left the tent and walked a short distance before stopping to talk. “I think we have to tell him everything. It’s our only way of getting out of this mess,” Adam said to Maggie.

“I know, honey, but I’m so worried about Angel. Will we be able to protect him?”

“We’ll do whatever needs to be done, Maggie. I know that our lives won’t be the same, but at least we won’t have to hide anymore. We can’t go on like this.”

They hugged, holding each other close for a moment and then walked back to join the others.

“Governor,” Adam began, “I did not steal any gold from Mr. Fitz or from the mines. The truth is that my son has a rare condition. His body turns food into gold during digestion, and he eliminates the gold the same way the rest of us eliminate the food we eat. It’s Angel’s gold.”

The Governor stared blankly at Adam, not understanding and getting a bit angry about it. He said, “What are you talking about?”

Adam added, “We can prove it, but first I guess it would be best if I let the Professor explain.”

The Professor proceeded to unfold the sequence of events, first reminding the Governor about the accident at the mine. “I do remember that,” Governor Tannin replied.

The Professor then described Adam’s injury, and his creation of the vaccine, which healed the leg but couldn’t eliminate the gold in Adam’s bloodstream.

He then recounted the test results when he examined both Maggie and Adam a few years later when they wanted to start a family.

All the while, the Governor was listening intently while staring at the Professor as he spoke.

"I created a vaccine which helped them conceive, and Maggie was able to give birth to a healthy baby boy."

Then the Professor went into detail explaining all the examination and test results for Angel, which confirmed his condition. As the Professor concluded, he said, "Governor, these are highly unusual circumstances, but nonetheless, true."

The Governor was stunned and could hardly believe what they were saying, but the Professor seemed so competent, so confident, when confirming his findings.

"You've made mistakes before, Professor, or don't you remember how you caused my daughter's death.

"And why are you even practicing medicine? I forbid you to practice medicine years ago," the Governor said, even though he knew it wasn't the Professor's fault. After all, Prudence had eaten when she wasn't supposed to.

The Professor was silent as he recalled the tragedy.

After thinking things through for a moment, the Governor turned to Adam and said, "This is a shocking situation, and you must understand that I will need to see proof."

"Of course, replied Adam. "I'll be right back."

Adam quickly returned with a small gold nugget. "This is from our son this morning."

The Governor took the nugget from Adam and examined it more closely. It was gold, he thought, but not in the usual shape of mined gold—it was rounded and more smooth.

"Can I keep this for further study?" asked the Governor.

"Yes, you can," Adam said, as the Governor slipped it into his pocket.

The Professor commented, "You'll see that this gold is more pure than the mined variety, which contains other minerals and composites from the earth."

"How do I know that this came from the boy?" the Governor asked. "I'd have to see it for myself. Where is the child?"

Adam turned to Maggie and said, "Honey, I think we should let him see."

Maggie agreed and said, "Okay, but Governor, you must assure us that once you see Angel, and we prove that we're telling the truth, all charges will be dropped against everyone, and the sale of the mountain will stand."

"I think that can be arranged," the Governor responded, anxious to see if this could possibly be true.

"Alright," Maggie said. "I'll go get him."

Maggie brought Angel in, and said, "Sweetheart, this is Governor Tannin. He's in charge of the whole State of California. Governor, this is our son, Angel."

The Governor was somehow surprised to see a normal, sweet-looking child—he didn't know what he was expecting—and he shook the boy's hand.

Later that afternoon, when Angel had to go, the Governor accompanied him and got his proof.

As incredible as it was, the Governor couldn't deny it and immediately began trying to convince Adam to let him take the boy.

"I'd take him to the finest scientists and physicians in the state—in the country, in fact."

But Adam interrupted him and firmly said, "Absolutely not!"

"The Professor is the only doctor Angel needs," Maggie added.

"Well, I will need to discuss this situation with Mr. Fitz and see if I can convince him of your innocence," the Governor replied.

The Governor left Mount Dove and headed back to town. He sent one of his aides to find Mr. Fitz. "Bring him to the mansion and tell him it's urgent."

When Fitz arrived at the Governor's mansion, Governor Tannin told him about all he had seen. Fitz didn't believe it—he was overwhelmed by the thought.

Tannin pulled the gold nugget from his pocket and handed it to his friend. Fitz stared at it for a long time, saying nothing. He started to pace around the room, rubbing the nugget in his hand, as his mind tried to comprehend the circumstances and sort it out. He began to mumble to himself and got more and more worked up as he reached his conclusion.

"It's all because of me," he said to himself. "It's all because of me."

He repeated himself several times as the realization crystallized. Then, he turned to his friend and said, "Don't you see, Jeffrey, it all happened because of me. Adam's accident happened on my property. The gold that infected him, that entered his system, was mine. And it was passed on to his son, which means the gold that comes from his son belongs to me, too. It's all mine."

The Governor was suddenly snapped out of his own thoughts and contemplated the series of events. As crazy as it sounded, the more he thought about it, the more it seemed to have some logic.

"You know, Andrew, you may have a point there."

"Well, of course I do. I'm telling you, that boy's gold belongs to me."

The Governor was quiet for a moment and then continued. "I think we can make a case for this—it's incredible, but it just may work."

Andrew Fitz was in his own world now, rubbing the nugget. His eyes widened as his brain was going over all the details, the progression of events, the possibilities for the future. "The possibilities for the future are enormous!" he stated emphatically to his friend.

"We need to get the boy, Jeffrey. How can we do that?" Fitz asked.

"I tried to get him on the pretense of taking him for medical treatment, but they wouldn't hear of it," the Governor replied.

"No one else knows about this, except for the people on the mountain, right?" Fitz asked.

"Yes, other than us—I was the first person to actually witness the boy when he . . . umm . . . you know," the Governor replied.

"Aren't they in violation of the court order?" Fitz asked.

"They will be by tomorrow at midnight," said the Governor.

"And the Chief is still on my mountain," Fitz continued. "I think we can call out the full army on this one, Jeffery. We can storm the mountain and grab the boy," Fitz concluded.

"I think you're right, Andrew, but it's a bit extreme. How would it look?"

"It's going to look like you're enforcing the law," Fitz responded.

Governor Tannin hesitated, but Fitz kept pressing him. "Don't forget who got you elected," Fitz added. "You must do this for me, Jeffery."

The Governor was concerned but also excited. He had never ordered the army before, and to command such a force, got him all pumped up.

As he thought it through, he became satisfied with the reasoning—it was a serious situation, and it justified the involvement of the troops.

"Everyone will understand," the Governor said, as he finished convincing himself. "I must enforce the law. The Indians bought the mountain with stolen gold."

"That's right," Fitz reassured him.

"And the arrest warrant must be enforced," the Governor added.

"Of course," Fitz agreed.

The Governor then sat in his chair and pushed a button under his desk; his aide instantly entered the room.

"Yes, Governor," the aide said.

"Send a message to Major Lemer to come see me immediately.

After Major Lemer arrived at the Governor's mansion and was fully briefed on the situation, he told the Governor that the army would need about a week to be fully ready to attack and secure the mountain.

The Governor then called his aide again and asked him to personally deliver a written message to the Chief.

When the Governor's aide arrived at Mount Dove, Wildwind took the letter and brought it to his father. It stated that the entire mountain had to be evacuated in seven days. Adam, and the Professor, and the Sisters would be arrested and given the opportunity of a trial by their peers. Maggie was added to the arrest warrant for aiding and abetting. And Angel was to be put under the supervision of the State of California—the Governor would personally see to his care.

Within hours after delivering the written directive, there was a movement of forces in the valley around Mount Dove. It was a build-up of army power, gradually increasing. They crossed the river of Valley Creek and began surrounding the mountain. The transfer of supplies between the tribe and the orphanage stopped—it was too dangerous to risk passage outside the Indian territory.

Chief North Star and Adam walked to the peak of the mountain where they could see the entire valley.

"It looks like we'll be outnumbered, Chief. We have less than eight hundred warriors, and they'd be fighting against a strong, well trained army. We won't have a chance."

"We may have fewer warriors," the Chief responded, "but we also have great determination. We are fighting for our homeland, and when one is forced to defend their home, great strength comes from within. Strategically, we hold the higher ground and know the terrain better than they do. We can attack with power as they approach; and with a hard first hit, we can cause them heavy casualties." He paused for a moment and continued, "That could force them to withdraw."

"Still, Chief," Adam replied, "many of your men will die, and if the troops don't back down, they could kill us all. The Governor is a proud man."

"A proud man, in this case, is a foolish man," said the Chief. "We must protect our land, our home."

"I think Mr. Fitz just wants the gold and my son," Adam said, "so if we leave and go far away, we can hide, and he will never find us. Maybe then he'd leave you alone."

"They will never leave us alone," the Chief replied. "Some of them, like Mr. Fitz and the Governor, will always want to see us dead or gone; and they will not stop until they have our land. Mr. Fitz has connections in many places, and he will find you wherever you go. He will take your son. What will you do then, Adam? It will be too late. Now is the time to defend ourselves. We are fighting for our lives—not just yours."

Both men were silent as they watched the soldiers set up camp below them. There were nearly three thousand men on horseback and on foot awaiting the command to take the mountain by force.

The Chief put his arm around Adam and said, "Come, let's go. I have asked to meet with the tribe's elders. The Professor, Sister Agatha, Sister Mary, and Maggie will be there, as well. We will decide what is best for everyone."

"The Governor has betrayed us," Maggie said, as the meeting began in the Chief's tent.

Sister Mary said, "How are we going to get supplies to the orphanage?"

Sister Agatha turned to the Chief and said, "How long will your provisions for the tribe last? Without being able to freely hunt and fish, Chief, how long can we hold out?"

Sister Mary added, "I don't believe we would get a fair trial."

"Tannin will turn the story anyway he wants to best suit himself," the Professor interjected. "I'm afraid to think of what may happen if he gets his hands on Angel."

"He would turn him over to those scientists he mentioned," Maggie added. "We can't let him do that, Adam."

They all spoke with great emotion, and panic started to set in. The Chief held up his hand to gently quiet the group. "We will have to fight to protect ourselves and for our right to stay on Mount Dove. We have no choice. We must prepare for battle."

CHAPTER 15

FAMOUS

As night fell, Sister Agatha left the campsite, accompanied by an Indian guide. She was wearing a pair of brown pants and a white shirt. She hadn't worn regular clothes in years—and never pants. Her habit was folded neatly in a shoulder bag slung across her chest.

The two made their way down the mountain by foot and waded through a shallow stream until they reached the waterfall. Sister Agatha stood there—it seemed there was nowhere to go. But the Indian scout simply continued, walking through the waterfall and disappearing behind the sheet of water. Sister Agatha followed without further hesitation.

Behind the waterfall was a cave that led to a secret underground tunnel, which ran under the river of Valley Creek. It was narrow, and, at some places, they had to crawl on their hands and knees. As they made their way, they could hear the river flowing above them.

Sister Agatha and the Indian guide continued to travel for a long time and finally got through to the other side, leaving the troops behind them.

As they emerged from the dark underground tunnel, they looked up and could see the stars and the full moon above, lighting their way. The breeze of the fresh night air felt good as it hit their faces.

They walked for a few more miles, until they finally arrived at a small cabin.

Two fresh horses were waiting for them, along with a change of clothes. Sister Agatha was happy to get out of her wet garments and put on a dark blue dress. She and the Indian guide mounted the horses and started to make their way to Sacramento.

They rode for a few hours before arriving at the Sacramento train station. She thanked her Indian guide before boarding the train to Missouri.

After more than eighteen hours on the train, she arrived at the Missouri train station. It was in the early morning hours, and she felt it was safe enough to send a telegram:

MR. PRESIDENT. URGENT. NEED HELP. COMING TO SEE YOU. ARRIVING TOMORROW NIGHT AT 8. SISTER AGATHA.

She quickly changed into her habit and headpiece and boarded the next train to Washington, D.C. She was on her way to see the President of the United States.

She was pleased that she and the President had stayed in touch since Adam and Maggie's wedding. He was a busy man, she knew, but she also knew him to be a fair and good man. She was certain he would help.

When she arrived in the Washington, D.C, train station, Sister Agatha was met by two army officers, who escorted her to a waiting carriage that took her directly to the White House. Before she had time to admire the beautiful décor and lavish furnishings, she was quickly ushered into the President's private office—a dark wood paneled library with floor-to-ceiling bookcases and rich leather seating.

The President entered the room from another doorway, and he rushed to greet her—hugging her like an old friend. "It's wonderful to see you again, Sister Agatha." He led her to the couch, and they sat down. "What is so urgent that it brings you here?"

Sister Agatha told the President all about the false accusations against Adam for stealing from the mines; the way the Professor had been jailed and how she had to get him out; and all about the Governor's orders. "Although he knows the truth," Sister Agatha said, "he's still ordered the troops to Mount Dove!"

When she told him about Mr. Fitz burning down the orphanage, the President commented, "I knew he was an evil man. I won't even shake that man's hand! He spread those awful rumors about Colonel Saunders during the California Governor's race a few years back. Colonel Saunders is a friend of mine and would have been an excellent and honest Governor."

Sister Agatha thought it best to tell the President everything, and when it came to explain about the gold, she told him about Angel's condition. This was the one part of her story that he could not believe. There would be time to check that out later, he thought, but for now, he had to act.

"It's certainly urgent, Sister, and I'm glad you came to see me. Time is short. I'll issue an override to the Governor's orders, but it will take a couple of hours to get it done."

The President got up, walked over to his desk, and rang a buzzer. An aide immediately knocked on the office door. "Come in," the President said. The aide walked toward the desk where the President was writing a note. He finished and handed it to the young man. "Deliver this to General Mersel, and please hurry."

"General Mersel will accompany you back to Mount Dove. Now, why don't you have a bite to eat, wash up, and rest. Then you can take a tour of the place while I get the paperwork going."

The President took Agatha's arm and led her out the door. A young man in uniform was standing there.

"Please see to Sister Agatha's needs."

"Yes, sir," the soldier replied.

"Thank you, Mr. President." She walked toward the smiling soldier and took his arm.

General Mersel was an honorable, dependable man. As soon as he received the President's note, he chose ten officers to accompany him to Mount Dove. Together they loaded horses and supplies on a special train provided for their journey. The President gave Sister Agatha a ride to the station in the presidential carriage, where they said their goodbyes. He handed the General his orders, and they boarded the train.

After three days on the train and a few hours ride on horseback, they were within a mile of the troops at the base of Mount Dove. When they finished the last-minute preparations, they began the final ride to the mountain.

Mount Dove was fully surrounded now. The attack would start soon. The number of soldiers who crossed the river of Valley Creek kept growing, and on horseback, they formed lines that were ten men across and twenty men deep. The troops started to march forward, in a synchronized stride. The sound of the horses hooves were all you could hear . . . a loud 'Clunk! Clunk! Clunk!'

Major Lemer looked out at the sea of dark blue uniformed men, the flag of the State of California was displayed proudly by the first soldier in the front line. He gave the order to raise their muskets, and shouted, "ATTACK!"

The Indians were entrenched in the mountain—their faces painted for war—and quietly waited for the soldiers to get closer. They had planned to create a diversion in the foothills of the mountain and draw the fire to one direction, while they attacked from another. They waited patiently and prepared for battle.

General Mersel and his men, with Sister Agatha riding at his side, were just a short distance away. The General looked through his binoculars. "It looks like they're beginning to advance."

Just then, shots rang out, and they could see that the troops were advancing up the mountain. "They've started already," Sister Agatha said.

One officer held up the flag of the President of the United States, another had the American flag, as they started to gallop as fast as they could toward Mount Dove. They were fully visible as soon as they passed the hillside.

One of Major Lemer's men directed his attention to the group as they were approaching from the distance. Major Lemer looked through his binoculars and was surprised to see the General and his officers heading toward the battle field, displaying the flag of the President of the United States. He rode quickly to greet them.

"Sir, I am General Mersel, and I am here on behalf of the President of the United States. I have an order, issued by the President himself, which commands you to immediately cease this aggression and disarm."

Major Lemer took the paperwork from the General and read it quickly. The order was clear; he had no choice. He turned to his first officer and said, "Blow the horn to retreat."

The troops stopped in their tracks. They were instructed to re-group at the bottom of the mountain and cross back over the river of Valley Creek, where the Major ordered them to return to the base. He saluted the General, tipped his hat to Sister Agatha, and turned to leave after the last of his men had gone.

General Mersel and his men followed Sister Agatha up the mountain, where an Indian scout led them to Chief North Star and the Tommahoe camp.

Everyone was so grateful to General Mersel and his men. The Chief welcomed them and made them all comfortable. They were invited to rest and stay for dinner; the Chief made it a feast for all.

The next day, the General began his official inquiry into the whole situation. He had been instructed by the President to do a thorough investigation so that the legal charges still issued against them by the Governor could be addressed.

General Mersel spoke to each person privately. He met first with Adam, who explained that he had been accused of stealing, while, in fact, the gold he had wasn't stolen at all. He went on to tell the General about his son, Angel, but when he couldn't explain all the scientific details, he suggested that the General speak with Professor Morgansteen.

The meeting with the Professor took half the day. The Professor explained to General Mersel how it all happened, scientifically, and how the condition began with Adam's fall in the mine. He showed the General how he produced the medicine in the lab he had set up at the Indian camp when he first arrived, and how the medication worked with Angel's body chemistry.

The General even witnessed Angel making his gold and was astonished. If he hadn't seen it with his own eyes, General Mersel would not have believed where the gold nuggets came from.

While the General conducted his investigation, word got out to the people of Goldstone about the happenings at Mount Dove, and it was the talk of the town. Curiosity brought folks to the mountain, and some newspaper reporters set up camp in the valley to stay close to the story.

Two days later, the General finished his report and sent his findings, by messenger, directly to the President.

News spread quickly and was first reported by the Sacramento Times.

The headline read, 'ANGEL OF GOLD.'

Newspapers around the country picked up on the story, and another front page read, 'THE BOY WHO POOPED GOLD.'

The Washington Press was the first to print excerpts of the General's official report. It was now the talk of the country.

The entire nation learned about the terrible actions of Andrew Fitz. It would be left up to Sister Agatha to bring charges against him for burning the orphanage.

Governor Tannin tried to keep a low profile and denied ever knowing anything other than what was told to him by Mr. Fitz.

General Mersel went on to recommend that Professor Morgansteen have his license to practice medicine reinstated. He also specified that any and all charges against Adam and Maggie Starks, Sister Agatha, Sister Mary, and the Professor be dropped immediately as they were unfounded.

The General also deemed the gold Chief North Star used to purchase Mount Dove to be legal tender, and the land was now to be officially registered as the property of the Chief and the Tommahoe Indian tribe.

The report went on to recommend that Angel Starks remain in the care of his parents.

All of General Mersel's recommendations were approved by the President, who sent a special request, along with the report, to the Supreme Court, asking for a speedy decision in its final ruling on the case.

The court decision came quickly, and they agreed with all of the recommendations as outlined in the General's summary.

General Mersel informed Adam and Maggie that the gold was legally theirs, and they could feel free to do with it as they wished.

Adam and Maggie knew exactly what they wanted to do with their fortune.

They purchased the farm property up north for the Sisters and built a new orphanage. As time went by, the number of children at the orphanage grew to over a hundred. And the farm was cultivated to produce enough earnings to support the orphanage on its own.

Adam bought his parents the farm his father had always dreamed about. James quit the mining business and planted grapevines, eventually operating a successful winery in northern California.

Mr. and Mrs. Davis were also taken care of, and the General Store was enlarged and updated.

For themselves, Adam and Maggie built a new house, right next door to the new home they built for Professor Morgansteen, which included a separate laboratory building.

The Professor continued to produce the medicine Angel needed while he worked on a cure for the boy. Angel was growing up beautifully and was in excellent health, except for the matter of the gold.

Adam and Maggie made arrangements for a portion of the gold to be transferred to currency and deposited on a regular basis in a fund that helped the poor.

Every Sunday, Adam and Maggie took Angel to their special place beneath the willow tree for a picnic. It became a Starks family tradition.

On one Sunday, Adam surprised Maggie again—this time with a gold wedding ring, placed on top of her sandwich—the same way he had proposed to her seven years earlier. It was the gold ring he had promised her when she agreed to marry him. The ring had a special wooden inlay that was hand-crafted by Mr. Loomis. The combination of the wood and gold was a reminder that in poor days and in rich days, they loved each other just as much.

There was peace on Mount Dove, and life was good in the town of Goldstone; although, once in a while, a reporter stopped by to check up on the progress of Angel of Gold.

The End